A VERY WITCHY YULETIDE

D. LIEBER

This is a work of fiction. Names, characters, places, and incidents either are the product of the author's imagination or are used fictitiously. Any resemblance to actual persons, living or dead, events, or locales is entirely coincidental.

Copyright © 2020 by D. Lieber

All rights reserved. No part of this book may be reproduced or used in any manner without written permission of the copyright owner except for the use of quotations in a book review. For more information, address: contact@inkandmagick.com

First paperback edition October 2020

Cover Design and Layout by Section 28 Publishing

Edited by Cover to Cover Editing

ISBN: 978-1-951239-08-4 (Hardcover Print)
ISBN: 978-1-951239-09-1 (Paperback Print)
ISBN: 978-1-951239-10-7 (Ebook)

Ink & Magick

www.inkandmagick.com

To my Pagan sisters and brothers. Blessed Be.

Special Thanks

As always, I would like to thank everyone who helped me research and beta this book. A special thanks to Joyce, Amy, Wren, Kass, Laura, Aunt Debbie, and John.

A NOTE FROM THE AUTHOR

Dear Reader,

Let me take you aside for a moment before you begin. While I am attached to all of my work, this story holds a particularly special place for me.

As someone who is Pagan and visually impaired, I have been pressured to share those aspects of my life in my writing for many years. People want to know what it's like. I understand. I found, to my surprise, that sharing those very personal experiences is much more difficult than I thought it would be. It puts me in a very vulnerable place.

The confrontations my characters experience in regards to their religion and Evergreen's visual impairment are all situations I have experienced in my own life. However, I did take some artistic license in regards to exact situation to better fit the story. This is by no means my autobiography. In fact,

Evergreen responds to many of these confrontations in a completely different way than I did myself.

I would also like to say that my experiences do not necessarily reflect the experiences of the people who are part of the same minorities as myself. I do not speak for all Pagans everywhere. My experiences with my own blindness do not necessarily reflect the experiences of the entire blind community. Both of those things are very personal and are experienced in a myriad of ways. These are but some of the situations I've dealt with in my personal life.

Thank you for taking the time to read this little note. I do hope sharing this story, and thus some of my personal experiences, will let you see the world from a slightly different angle.

Your support is much appreciated, as always.

D. Lieber

CHAPTER 1

*E*vergreen took a deep breath and tapped the submit button, sending her sparse résumé off to another company that wasn't likely to hire her. Placing her tablet on the coffee table before her, she ignored the building anxiety in her chest.

She grabbed her tea from the table, the fabric of her sweatshirt protecting her fingers from getting burned by the hot ceramic. Tucking her legs under her on the couch, she looked out at the bright, snowy morning. The snow dusted the naked tree limbs of the woods outside her apartment window, and little icicles glistened in morning sunshine.

Muir sat tall on the windowsill, his striped tail twitching as he squinted at some busy, morning birds.

Evergreen's apartment was unusually quiet this morning, her roommate having gone home for the holidays. Most of the building was quiet in fact, due to the amount of college residents. It was the pleasant silence of solitude where she could just sit, drink tea, and watch her cat.

The stillness was broken with a loud chiming melody. She jumped when her cellphone rang, hissing as hot tea seeped into the cloth of her sweatshirt and pajama pants.

She put the cup back on the table and answered the phone without seeing who was calling.

"Hello?" she said, clicking her tongue at having made a mess.

"What's wrong?" her mom asked.

"Nothing. I just spilled some tea."

"Are you all right?"

"Yeah, I'm fine. What's up?"

"Well, I know you said you weren't going to come home for break because you wanted to look for jobs, but I'm calling to ask you to reconsider."

Evergreen frowned. "I know I've always come home for Yule before, but I only have one semester left until I graduate. Between helping with preparations and taking care of the guests, it's just too busy there."

"I know, but I really think coming home would be good for you. I can tell you're stressed. You still have an entire semester to look for jobs, and being around family would help you relax."

Evergreen hesitated.

"And I called to tell you we're doing something special this year," her mom added.

"Yeah? What's that?"

"Well, as it's been a while since we've all gotten together, your dad and I talked with the old coven, and everyone has decided to come for a visit."

Evergreen's heart jumped. "Everyone...? Do you even have space for everyone?"

"Well, not everyone. I doubt Charlie will come. We don't have any retreats scheduled, so we can make room, even if you kids have to put sleeping bags on the floor."

"You're *really* convincing me," Evergreen answered, rolling her eyes.

"Oh, stop. It's been so long since we've all been together. It won't be the same if you aren't there. Won't it be nice to see everybody?"

Her answering silence was heavy. *Yes, it would be nice to see everyone,* Evergreen thought. It had been a long time since the old coven had all been in the same place. What with life being as it is, the families had moved away one by one.

A Yuletide with everyone there sparked joyful memories. So many sabbats happily celebrating the seasons. Of course she wanted that nostalgic feeling again. But things were different now. She was different. Evergreen bit her lip and twisted the end of one sleeve between her hands. *Can I even handle it?* she wondered.

"Is...is he...?" she started to ask.

"Yes," her mother answered. "Sawyer will be here, too."

Evergreen's chest tightened, and warmth spread through her. "I don't know, Mom..." she murmured.

Her mom's voice softened into that soothing tone only mothers can manage. "You'll be all right," she promised. "It has been what? Almost five years since you last saw him? You're a different woman now. Think of all you've seen, experienced, accomplished. Surely you aren't still carrying a torch for him, are you? After all this time, how many boys have you dated since then?"

"A few."

"And you did just fine with them. Don't let an old crush get in the way of us having a happy Yule."

"You're right." Evergreen nodded curtly and straightened her spine. "It was just a silly schoolgirl crush. It's not like he ever even noticed. And I've had good relationships since then, even if they didn't turn out. I'm not the same insecure girl who used to watch him. And you know what? He's probably not the same either. He's probably nothing like the boy I knew."

"That's right," her mom encouraged. "It will just be old friends getting together for the holiday," she promised.

Evergreen smiled. "That sounds nice."

"So you'll come?"

"Yeah, just let me pack my bags and get Muir in his carrier. I'll be there by dinnertime."

Her mom let out a soft squeak. "I'm so happy you reconsidered. Be careful. Okay? I'll see you later."

"I will. Love you, Mom."

"I love you, too."

After hanging up the phone, Evergreen sat for a moment. Anxiety swirled in her gut, but she squashed it down. *I can do this. No problem,* she thought.

After dumping what was left of her now cold tea into the sink, she went and scooped up Muir. She stood at the window, the morning sun bright but distant as it hit her face. Holding Muir like a baby, she kissed him on his little forehead. "Come on, Muir. Let's get ready, eh? I'm going to pack your favorite toy and treats. I'll make sure to put your warm, fuzzy blanket in your carrier. You better behave yourself. No fighting with Larkspur and no attacking the Yule tree. I'm going to put your special Yule collar on you. We've got to make you all handsome to see everyone. We're going home, Muir."

CHAPTER 2

Sawyer could feel his cellphone silently vibrating in the pocket of his jeans, but he just let it ring as he concentrated on bottle-feeding the baby bat, which was wrapped in a towel in the crook of his arm.

"There's a good girl," he murmured to the little creature as she hungrily sucked on the bottle. "Good job," he praised.

After putting the pup back with her siblings, he washed his hands and pulled his phone from his pocket. He'd missed a call from his mom.

As he headed to the breakroom, he held and pressed the two on his screen. While the speed-dial connected, he poured himself some coffee from the communal pot.

"Why didn't you answer?" his mom asked once she'd picked up.

"I'm at work, Mom. What's up?"

"I thought you had the day off."

"Well…they were short-handed."

His mom clicked her tongue. "Aren't they always?"

"Come on, Mom. Don't be like that. The animals need to be taken care of."

"Are you still going to be able to come home for Yule?"

"Yeah, no problem. It was only today they needed extra help."

"Well, that's all right then."

"Did you need something? Or did you just call to chat?"

"There's been a change of plans."

Sawyer frowned into his coffee. He didn't like when his mom got that conspiratorial tone in her voice. But he waited for her to continue.

"Ria called. She and Wes invited everyone to come and stay with them for the holiday. I told them we would both be there."

Sawyer froze, his heart pounding hard in his chest. But he didn't speak; he'd always relied on silence to hide his emotions in situations such as this.

"Eeva will be there," his mom continued, hitting the exact point he both longed to know and dreaded to hear. "Ria tells me she's close to graduating with her Bachelor's. Did you know she goes to the college near you?"

Sawyer cleared his throat. "No, I didn't know," he lied.

His mind flashed with images from his youth: Eeva all in white at Imbolc, Eeva dancing around the Maypole at Beltaine, Eeva sitting with her back to a tree and her nose buried in a book. He'd never been brave enough to tell her how he'd felt. Animals and plants were much more his speed. The trees didn't care if you stumbled over your words.

Had she been sad when he'd gone so far away to school? He'd always wondered. But she'd never called or texted. She'd never messaged him on social media. She'd never even emailed. It's not as if she hadn't known how to find him if she'd wanted to. He remembered the last time he'd seen her. She sat on the steps of his porch, her elbows on her knees and her head in her hands as she stared at the oak tree in his front yard. She'd only looked at him for a moment as he called his goodbyes before her parents and his mom had embraced him, wishing him well on his way to the freshman dorms three states over.

"Sawyer, are you listening to me?" his mom shouted into his ear, drawing him from his memories.

"I'm sorry. What did you say?"

She sighed dramatically. "I said Ria told me she's single right now."

His chest squeezed. "So?" he managed.

"You can't fool your mom, mister. I know how you've always felt about her."

"That was a long time ago."

She blew a raspberry into the phone. "Uh-huh and those perfectly nice girls you dated in college? Shelby and Michelle and what was her name?"

"Krystal," he supplied.

"Right, and Krystal. What was wrong with them? I didn't push you at the time because I knew the problem."

His face flushed, dreading what she was about to say.

"They weren't Eeva. That's what," she finished. "And now you have the chance, and all you can say to me is 'so?' as if it all has nothing to do with you?"

"What do you want me to do, Mom?" Sawyer snapped. His

stomach clenched in immediate regret.

"You're not the same scared little boy anymore, Sawyer. You've done a lot since you went away. You graduated college and got a job doing what you love. I've seen you grow into a good and confident man. But as wonderful as you are, son, you can't expect everything to just come to you like a stray cat you've coaxed into trusting you. Sometimes, you do have to put in a little bit of effort and go after what you want. Show her who you are. Tell her how you feel."

"It *has* been a long time. And you're right, I've changed a lot. But don't you think she's changed, too? She's probably nothing like the Eeva I knew."

"Well, there's only one way to find out. Are you going to let that uncertainty get in the way? Come to the gathering. You don't have to do anything right off. Spend some time together; see how you both have changed. Maybe you'll find you like her even more now."

"You know what? You're right. There's no pressure after all this time. Maybe I'll find I like her more, and I'll finally have the courage to tell her. But it's also possible I won't like her at all anymore, and I can finally move on. This is a good idea."

He could hear the smile in his mom's voice when she responded. "Excellent. So, after work you'll come home? Then, you can spend the night here, and we can go there tomorrow morning."

Sawyer nodded. "Sounds good."

"Wonderful. Love you bunches."

"Love you, too, Mom. Bye."

After his phone beeped in his ear, Sawyer stood in the relative silence of the wildlife refuge's breakroom, the only sounds the humming of the refrigerator and the distant chirps, squeaks, and squawks of the animals in their care. Closing his eyes, he let out a long sigh to steady his nerves. *I can do this. No problem,* he thought.

CHAPTER 3

Evergreen smiled to herself as the train slowed down, pulling into the Main Street station of Birchland. Holiday decorations sparkled and twinkled in every storefront window. The huge tree in the town square was already alight as the early sunset of winter hugged the western horizon.

After slinging her backpack over her shoulders—double checking to ensure her cane was folded inside—she pulled her luggage down from the overhead compartment. Then, she hurriedly grabbed Muir's carrier, knowing the train wouldn't be stopping at the station for very long. Still, she was careful as she walked past the seated passengers, not wanting to hit them with anything.

On the platform, Muir meowed his complaints as the cold wind blew through the holes of his carrier.

"I know, baby boy," she soothed. "I will call for a ride right now."

Evergreen dug her cellphone out of her back pocket and

pulled up the ridesharing app. She went about ordering a ride and headed to the front of the station.

Muir cried pitifully again.

"Don't worry," she told him. "It says our driver will be here in four minutes. Then you will be in the nice warm car."

A few minutes later, a light blue car pulled up to the curb. The door opened, and a man stepped out. He wasn't much taller than Evergreen, but what he lacked in height he made up for in good looks and fashion sense. His charcoal peacoat was pristine over his straight-legged jeans and clean, leather boots.

"Are you Niko?" Evergreen asked, trying to place the name the app had given her.

"Yes." His dark eyes glinted in his olive face, and his curly, black hair moved only slightly as he nodded at her. "You must be Evergreen," he said, his voice rich and smooth.

She nodded in turn.

"Let me help you with your bags," he offered, holding out his hand for her roller suitcase.

"Oh, yeah. Also, I have a cat. I hope that's okay."

"No problem. I love cats."

Evergreen followed Niko to his trunk and took off her backpack as he lifted her suitcase into it. She surreptitiously checked the license plate, comparing it to the one the app had provided. Then, she climbed into the passenger seat.

As he got behind the wheel, Niko looked over at Muir's carrier in Evergreen's lap, lowering his head so he could see through the gate.

"He's a cutie," Niko said.

Evergreen smiled. "Thank you."

Niko pulled away from the curb. "So, you're going up to the retreat center? What sort of retreat are they having this time?"

"You know it?"

"Of course. I take guests up there all the time."

Evergreen nodded. "They aren't having a retreat. My parents own it. I'm just coming home for the holidays."

"Ah."

A few blocks away, they were out of the main part of town and on the winding road engulfed by snow-laden trees. Evergreen pushed her sunglasses up onto her head, the car too dark with the added shade. She glanced over at Niko, now a silhouette against the outside light.

"Have you lived in Birchland long?" Evergreen asked.

"How do you know I'm not from here?" He sounded like he was smirking.

I'd remember a guy like you, Evergreen thought. "Well...I don't know everyone, but there's only one high school in town. And you don't look that much older than me. Unless...did you go to Birchland Catholic?"

He nodded. "I did, though I took an elective summer class at Birchland High once. You're looking at someone who survived twelve years of Catholic school. I've lived here my whole life, except for the summers I spent visiting family in Greece."

"That must have been fun."

"It was," Niko agreed. "What year did you graduate? 2017? 2018?"

"2016. You?"

"2015."

"I had a...friend who graduated that year, but he went to Birchland High."

"Yeah? What's his name?"

"Sawyer Collins."

"Collins, Collins," he muttered, searching to place the name. "It sounds familiar…Oh! Was he a tall guy, kind of quiet, with wavy blond hair and brown eyes? Yeah, I think he was in that summer photography class. He didn't really talk much, but man his nature photography was amazing."

They're amber not brown, Evergreen thought. "Yeah, he was really into photography. That probably was him."

Niko glanced over at her with a grin. "Look at that," he said. "Birchland is a small town after all."

Her skin tingled as his suave tone caressed it.

"What's Collins doing now?"

"I don't know. I haven't talked to him in a long time. But he's supposed to be coming in for the holiday, so maybe you'll run into him."

"Yeah, maybe. Well, here we are," Niko said, pulling into the round drive of The Spiral Path Retreat Center and parking.

They both got out of the car and went back to the trunk. Niko placed Evergreen's suitcase on the ground beside her then hooked her backpack onto the extended handle.

"Well, if you ever need a ride, you know how to find me," he said with that easy tone.

She nodded. "Thank you. Happy holidays."

"You too, Evergreen. See you around."

Evergreen could feel his lingering gaze as he flashed her a smooth smile. Her cheeks warmed. Niko gave her a polite nod, got back into his car, and drove away.

She shook herself. *Gods, he was pretty,* she thought. Even though she knew he was only nice to her to get a good rating, she didn't even care. It felt good when a hot man smiled and called her name, but she had no delusions that he was attracted to her. She could tell the difference. Besides, she'd gone twenty-two years without ever seeing Niko. It wasn't likely she'd ever see him again.

As she turned toward the sturdy lodge, the calm warmth of home and hearth settled into her. Grabbing Muir's carrier and her roller suitcase, Evergreen headed up the wooden steps and in through the front door without knocking.

"I'm home!" she called as she closed the door behind her.

The cadence of small feet running on the wood floor approached her. Evergreen tensed for impact, placing Muir's carrier on the ground, as Sol rounded the corner.

"Eeva!" the little boy squealed.

Evergreen knelt to better catch the child as he launched himself into her arms.

"Hey there, Sparkler," she said, embracing him. "How did you get here before me? You must have learned how to fly."

He giggled, pulling away from her. "You're silly. Witches can't fly."

Evergreen tilted her head with a grin. "Are you sure about that?"

He nodded.

She reached out and tickled his belly. "Really sure?" she challenged through his giggling squeals.

"Yes," he screamed his answer.

"Well then. I've got news for you, sir." She picked him up, holding him by his middle tucked against her side like a football. She spun around, making zooming sounds as he laughed, his arms held out like Superman.

Slightly out of breath, Evergreen returned Sol to his feet. "See?" she said. "You flew."

"Do it again!" he demanded.

Just as she smiled, wondering if she had the endurance to pick the boy up for another go, his mother came around the corner.

"What's all this noise?" Cassandra asked, her voice smiling.

"Eeva was teaching me to fly," Sol explained.

"She was?" his mother asked. "Well, why don't you fly to the bathroom and wash your hands for dinner?"

The boy looked back up at Evergreen. "You're coming too?"

Evergreen smiled. "I'll be right there," she promised.

And Sol was gone just as fast as he'd come.

Evergreen embraced Cassandra. "Hey, cuz," she murmured.

"Hey. Glad you made it safe. Aunt Ria was starting to worry."

"Starting? When isn't she already?"

Cassandra chuckled.

"I can't believe how big he's gotten," Evergreen commented.

"I know. He's growing so fast. Almost five already. But, you know, it wouldn't be so much of a shock if you came around more often."

"Yeah, yeah. I hear you. It will be easier when I'm done with school."

Cassandra nodded and picked up Muir's carrier. "Is your mama still spoiling you, Muir?" she asked the cat, peering in at him.

"He's not spoiled. He's just loved. You have your baby, and I have mine."

"Aunt Ria already put the spare litter box in your room. Do you need help carrying this stuff upstairs?"

"No, thanks. I can handle it," Evergreen responded.

Evergreen headed up the stairs to the third floor where her attic bedroom had been. She pulled up short when she opened the door. Even though she knew none of her things were there anymore since she'd taken them to her apartment, it was still jarring to see her familiar space turned into the cozy but impersonal visage of a guest bedroom.

Evergreen let Muir out of his crate and showed him where the litter box was. After he'd hopped out, she cradled him in her arms and headed downstairs.

"Wow," she murmured as she entered the common room.

The mantle of the fireplace was covered in greenery. The small flickering lights among the green said there were also candles. A fire crackled in the hearth.

The Yule tree in the corner was bright with string lights, and the heavy fragrance of cinnamon drifted in the air, emanating from the scented pinecones that hung among the branches.

"We did good, right?" her mom said, coming from the direction of the kitchen.

"It's beautiful," Evergreen complimented, crossing the room and kissing her mom on the cheek.

"I'm so glad you decided to come, baby girl," her mother said.

"Where's Dad?"

"In the kitchen. Dinner should be done in a few minutes."

"Here, hold your grandcat while I go say hi." Evergreen handed Muir into her mother's arms.

He purred as his grandma scratched his ears.

"Something smells good," Evergreen announced upon entering the large kitchen.

"There she is," her dad said, looking over his shoulder as he stood at the stove. "How was the ride?"

Evergreen stood on her tiptoes and kissed her dad on the cheek. "Not bad. Muir wasn't happy for the first hour, but he eventually fell asleep."

Her dad nodded. "You hungry?"

"Starving."

"Well, you're just in time. Why don't you help Mom set the table?"

"You got it."

The quiet family dinner was anything but. Every few minutes, a pair of fuzzy bodies tore through the dining room while Muir and Larkspur chased each other. Cassandra punctuated the scramble by scolding Sol every time he moved to join in the race. When ten minutes had passed with no sight of them, Evergreen got up, concerned about their silence.

"Muir?" she called, her tone laced with warning. "You better be behaving yourself."

Evergreen stalked through the house, her eyes scanning for her mischievous cat.

She found Larkspur seated at the base of the Yule tree just staring into the branches. She squinted at it, creeping closer as she searched, the lights too bright for her to make out anything dark.

"Muir!" she shouted.

The cat's yellow eyes, pupils wide, stared out at her from the branches of the tree.

"Get out of there, right now," she demanded.

He didn't move.

She reached toward him, and he jumped out of the tree, running to the safety of some dark corner where she couldn't reach him. Larkspur still sat at the foot of the tree, watching the exchange as though he couldn't be bothered.

"You're a bad influence," she said to her cat-sibling. Evergreen sighed and returned to the table. "These cats," she said, shaking her head as she sat back down.

CHAPTER 4

"Are you sure it's not too early?" Sawyer asked his mom as they drove up the winding road to the retreat center.

"I told Ria last night we'd be coming in early," she answered from the passenger seat of his car, wrapped in her hat, coat, scarf, and mittens while snuggled into a blanket. The heater was blaring so high that Sawyer had taken off his winter things and just wore his T-shirt and jeans.

"Besides, she knows how traffic makes me nervous. She told us to let ourselves in," she added.

He pulled into the round drive and parked behind a blue Honda he didn't recognize. The bumper sticker proudly proclaimed that the owner was a "Tree Loving Dirt Worshiper." Sawyer smiled, knowing he was in the right place.

It had been years since he'd been to the Pendre's house, but it looked just the same as he remembered. He glanced over at his mother as she struggled to free herself from her many layers.

He chuckled at her. "Do you need some help, Mom?"

She sighed. "No, I just can't seem to—ugh, it's like quicksand!"

He laughed harder. "Let me help you."

She glared at him. "Are you laughing at me, son?"

He tried to smother his smile. "Maybe. You know, if we had gotten in a crash, I bet you wouldn't even be injured with all your layers of cushion."

She scowled, though she had to be used to him teasing her for always being cold by now.

"Do you want my help?"

"No," she said proudly without bite. "I can do it myself."

"All right. Whatever you say," he said mockingly.

She pursed her lips. "Just go."

He moved around to the trunk and grabbed their luggage. As he closed the trunk, he peered through the back window at her. She had just extricated herself from the blanket and was struggling with her scarf. He shook his head, snickering to himself, and went on ahead.

Sawyer opened the front door as quietly as he could. It wasn't super early, but people did tend to sleep in while they were on vacation. He didn't want to disturb anyone.

He took the bags through the entrance hall and stopped in the living room. *I don't know what rooms we're staying in,* he thought. *We can just hang out here until someone gets up.*

He glanced around the room, cold and still in the early morning light. Evergreen boughs and ivy twisted among beeswax pillar candles on the mantle above the hearth. The

Yule tree in the corner was alight with crystal-style string lights, which danced on the holly berries and bells hung on the tree. Cinnamon scented pinecones were nestled in the branches.

Feeling something against his legs, Sawyer looked down at the grey tabby as it rubbed up against him, trilling. He smiled at the cat and crouched, holding out his hand so the animal could smell him.

It trilled again and purred. Sawyer picked it up, scratching its ear to the cat's sounds of delight.

"Muir!" A shout came from the direction of the kitchen. "I swear to all the gods, you better not be in that Yule tree."

Sawyer looked up just as Eeva stopped short upon entering the living room. She was still in her pajamas: flannel plaid pants with an oversized hoodie and fuzzy socks. Her long, brown hair was dyed a dark green, and it was still messy from sleep.

His heart throbbed in his chest, and he held his breath as he met her deep ocean blue eyes. His memories hadn't done her justice.

"Hey," he said lamely. "It's uh...been a while." He cleared his throat, his own voice sounding hoarse and uneven in his ears.

She blinked as if she'd forgotten who he was then frowned. "Yeah, I suppose that happens in life... How is...everything? I mean, I hope you and your mom are doing all right." Her tone was distant and polite. Formal.

His stomach clenched as his raised hopes deflated. "Yeah, everything's fine. We're both good. And you?"

"Same."

As the strained silence grew between them, Sawyer grasped for something to say. Anything. "So...my mom says you're graduating soon. What are you studying?" He knew very well she was studying history. It didn't matter that he'd said more times than he could count that he didn't care. The moment his mother mentioned her, he'd always internalized the information. And he'd taken more than a few glances at her social media profiles over the years, though he'd gotten better about that.

"Eeva!" his mother called, entering the room before they could struggle on in their conversation.

Eeva smiled, her eyes alight with the same warmth and kindness he'd seen so many times in his youth. "Tara," she said as his mother embraced her tightly. "It's so good to see you."

His mom held her at arms' length. "Let me get a good look at you." She clicked her tongue in a sound of appreciation. "Oh, still as beautiful as ever."

A light blush dusted Eeva's cheeks. *She still gets embarrassed by compliments*, Sawyer thought.

"Thank you," Eeva murmured.

"I love the hair color by the way," his mom continued. "Isn't she gorgeous, Sawyer? She's grown up a lot in the last four and a half years."

He ducked his head toward the purring cat in his arms, automatically falling into his old routine of silence and self-consciousness.

But unlike while he was growing up, his mother didn't just continue on with the conversation like the question was rhetorical, allowing him to stay comfortable in his shyness. Her silence was heavy as she stared at him expectantly.

He remembered their earlier conversation about how much he'd changed, how he needed to show Eeva who he was now, show her that confidence he'd gained over the years. He looked up at Eeva again, but she wasn't looking at him.

He let himself smile that smile he'd always kept to himself, that smile that had been too telling for him ever to let Eeva see.

"As ever," he said with a nod.

Eeva's eyes snapped to his. Her face flushed, and she looked away. "That's not very nice. After all this time, you catch me off guard in my PJs and then you tease me?" She pursed her lips, clearly displeased.

But before he could tell her he wasn't joking, she approached him, took the cat from his arms, and started from the room. "You guys make yourselves at home. Mom and Dad should be up before long, and they can tell you where to put your stuff. There's coffee and tea in the kitchen. I have to feed Muir and get ready."

CHAPTER 5

Evergreen could still feel her face flushed with heat as she shut her bedroom door behind her and placed Muir on the floor in front of his already full bowl. She rushed to the mirror above the dresser, leaning far over so she could properly see. She groaned at her disheveled appearance, finger-combing her messy hair and trying to smooth it into some semblance of order.

"Why did he have to get here so early?" she murmured.

Her stomach grumbled, reminding her that she'd left her breakfast mostly uneaten in the kitchen. She scowled at her reflection. "He didn't have to tease me. The old Sawyer never would have done that. Then again…the old Sawyer didn't talk much at all let alone smile mockingly and make rude comments."

Disappointment tingled across her skin before she could brush it aside. "That's good. I'm glad he's so different. Now, I won't have to worry about getting over him again. I've met tons of guys like that in the last few years. I know how to deal with them. No problem. Right, Muir?"

Muir's only answer was to crunch his kibble, his face shoved into his food bowl.

"Right," Evergreen answered for him.

She left her cat to his breakfast and grabbed her shower bag from her suitcase. Then, she went down the hall to the bathroom to get properly ready for visitors.

After putting on thick leggings, a black skirt and tank top, and her favorite upcycled sweater jacket, Evergreen smiled at her presentable appearance in her bedroom mirror just as a knock sounded the door.

"Come in," she called.

"Oh, don't you look cute," her mother said from the doorway.

"Thanks, Mom. What's up?"

"Would you come downstairs and help Tara and Sawyer get settled into their rooms?"

Evergreen quirked an eyebrow. "It's not like they haven't been here tons of time before. Why do they need help?"

Her mother pursed her lips. "Because they're our guests, Evergreen, and it's the polite thing to do."

"Fine," Evergreen sighed.

Her mom's voice smiled like she hadn't just been scolding her. "And your father is making omelets."

"All right. I'm coming." Evergreen left her door slightly open so Muir could get in and out when he wanted to and headed downstairs.

On the second-floor landing, she met her cousin, who smirked at her.

"Don't we look adorable this morning?" Cassandra said with a teasing tone that had way too much subtext.

Evergreen flipped her hair to one shoulder. "Hashtag woke up this way."

Cassandra laughed. "Uh-huh. I bet."

Back in the living room, Tara and Sawyer waited for their room assignments.

"Tara, I'm going to put you on the second floor. You'll be sharing with Hazel when she arrives," Ria told her.

"I guess Charlie isn't up for Yule," Tara said.

"Yeah, I think one Pagan is as much as he can handle. He's going to spend Christmas with his family," Ria agreed.

Tara nodded.

Evergreen reached for Tara's bag, but Cassandra got there first. Evergreen squinted at her cousin, who smiled innocently back before leading Tara to the second floor.

"And Sawyer, I'm sorry. But there just isn't enough room for everyone. Do you mind being in a sleeping bag in the meditation room?" Ria asked.

"Not at all, Ria," Sawyer answered, grabbing his suitcase.

Ria nudged Evergreen with her elbow, and Evergreen sighed and stepped closer to Sawyer.

"I can take your bag," Evergreen muttered.

"Oh, it's fine. I can carry it."

"Really, my mom is going to complain at me if I don't do it, so just give it here."

Her mom pretended like she didn't hear. "Go on, Sawyer. Evergreen will show you to your room. And she'll get the sleeping bag from the closet for you."

There was a heavy pause before Sawyer silently held out his

bag. As she took it from him, their fingers brushed together. Evergreen froze as a jolt ran through her. She glanced up at Sawyer. His amber eyes met hers below the soft waves of his golden hair.

"Well, go on," her mother urged. "Only a week and a half until Yule, and we still have a lot to do before then."

Evergreen felt her cheeks heat. She looked away, glaring at whatever her gaze landed on. "Come on," she said irritably as she started toward the meditation room.

At the far end of the house was a sunroom with glass walls trimmed in cedar and a peaked glass roof. Its wooden floor was empty save for an altar at the far end and shelves with rolled up yoga mats, blocks, and pillows near the door.

The scents of pine and cinnamon wafted through the air, coming from smoking incense on the altar. The altar had a wooden dish of salt, a crystal bowl of water, a white pillar candle—which flickered dimly in the morning light—and a small bucket of sand where the incense stuck out. The center of the altar had a foot-tall statue of the triple moon goddess, her long hair flowing down from her crown with the triple moon symbol on top. Her carved garments of green soapstone gracefully held the base of a flickering tealight. There was a conspicuous spot beside her, empty of the god statue that would soon return to its rightful place upon the god's rebirth on Yule.

Evergreen placed Sawyer's bag on the floor. "I'll go get your sleeping bag," she muttered.

She turned to leave as quickly as she could, but Sawyer called out to her. "Eeva," he said, his tone clipped as he tried to stop her before she was out of earshot.

She looked over her shoulder, raising an eyebrow at him.

"Thank you." His voice was warm and welcoming, and Evergreen just knew he was mocking her.

She squinted at him and left without a word. Digging through the hall closet in search of a sleeping bag, Evergreen jumped when her mother spoke from behind her.

"Is he getting settled?" she asked.

"How should I know?" Evergreen grumbled. "I put his stuff down in the meditation room, and now I'm trying to find the sleeping bags."

"Would it hurt you to be a little kinder in your tone, Evergreen? After all, the rule of three would still apply even if it wasn't the season to be *extra* kind to others," she lectured.

Evergreen sighed; her mother always used three-fold retribution as a way to curb bad behavior. "Yeah, yeah. Ah! Here they are. Finally." She pulled out an orange sleeping bag and stuffed the rest back as the lot surged toward her. Then, she quickly shut the closet door before they could change their minds about staying put.

"Take this as well." Her mother held out a space heater to her. "It's cold out there, especially at night."

"Fine," she agreed, heading back to the meditation room with her quest items.

CHAPTER 6

An unfamiliar feeling came over Sawyer as Eeva glared at him before turning to go find his sleeping bag. He'd never seen that defiant look in her eyes, at least not directed at him. She'd always been so warm, so bright and joyful before.

But she'd looked directly at him. She'd met his gaze straight on. And even though she was clearly irritated, for that moment, her attention was fully his.

Of course that wasn't the look he wanted from her. But it was a strong, personal reaction, and it belonged to him.

Eeva returned shortly with a sleeping bag and a space heater. She placed them near the door.

"Thank you, Eeva. And you even brought a heater. That's considerate of you." He smiled.

She squinted at his sincerity. "My mom gave it to me to bring."

"Still, you brought it." Sawyer didn't let his smile slip.

"Do you need anything else, or can I go eat my breakfast now?"

"Of course. I'm right behind you."

Sawyer followed Eeva through the house and into the kitchen, where her dad was standing at the stove making omelets.

Wes smiled over his shoulder at them. "Toppings are on the island," he told them. "Grab a bowl and fill it with what you want."

Sawyer stood beside Eeva, edging along the island, bowl in hand. The surface was covered with bowls of mushrooms, tomatoes, cheese, cubed ham, bacon, potatoes, bell peppers, and everything you'd ever want in an omelet. An odd addition caught Sawyer's eye. At the very center of the island was a mug of cocoa, its whipped cream deflated from sitting too long, and a piece of buttered toast topped with cinnamon and sugar, a neat bite taken out of one corner.

Sawyer smiled to himself. *Maybe she hasn't changed so much after all.*

After passing her additions to her dad, Eeva went on through to the dining room.

"It's been a while since we've all been together," Wes said to him, pulling Sawyer's attention away from Eeva's retreat.

"It has," Sawyer agreed.

"A lot has changed," Wes continued.

Sawyer nodded slowly, placing his bowl on the counter beside the cook.

They were silent for a moment, the only sound the sizzling hiss from the frying pan.

"Do you still keep your cocoa in the same place?" Sawyer asked.

Wes nodded, pointing his spatula to the cupboard above the coffee pot.

Sawyer went to the cupboard and took the glass jar of cocoa down along with a mug. After spooning a few heaping tablespoons into the cup, he poured hot water atop the powder from the electric kettle and stirred. Then, he went to the refrigerator, scanning the shelves.

"In the door," Wes instructed.

Sawyer grabbed the can of whipped cream from the door and squeezed a mound of it atop the cocoa. After returning the cocoa jar to the cupboard, he pulled down another with mini chocolate chips. He sprinkled the chips onto the whipped cream and grabbed the mug.

As Sawyer left the kitchen, he heard Wes mutter to himself. "Then again, maybe not so much after all."

In the dining room, his mom, Ria, Eeva, and Cassandra sat at the large table, waiting for breakfast. His mom warmed her hands on a cup of green tea while Ria and Cassandra had coffee.

They were chatting about all the things that needed to be done before Yule as he entered. He approached the table and sat in the empty seat beside Eeva, placing the mug of cocoa carefully before her.

She looked up at him, her eyebrows raised. "What's this?" she asked.

He smiled. "Cocoa."

Eeva lowered her gaze to the table, biting her lower lip ever so slightly. "Thank you," she mumbled.

His smile widened. "You're welcome."

"I'm most worried about the Yule log," Ria said, continuing her conversation without noticing their exchange.

"You didn't get it at Midsummer?" Tara asked.

Ria shook her head. "Everything else I either have or can get at the craft store if needed. Though I suppose we can go to the hardware store if we really can't find one."

Tara nodded. "Well, maybe one of the others will bring a log. You never know. When do they arrive?"

"Thursday, during the full moon," Ria answered.

"Don't worry, Aunt Ria," Cassandra said. "We still have plenty of time. And everyone will be here to help."

Sawyer felt a tug on his sleeve and looked over. A small boy, no older than five, stood beside him.

"You're in my seat," the child informed him.

Sawyer raised his eyebrows. "Am I?"

The boy nodded.

"I'm sorry about that. Just so I don't make that mistake again. How will I know it's yours in the future?" Sawyer whispered politely.

The child nodded, accepting his apology. "Because I always sit next to Eeva."

"Oh, but what if I want to sit next to Eeva?"

Eeva snorted into her cocoa then coughed. Everyone looked at her to make sure she was all right. She held up her hand to say she was, whipped cream smeared on her nose and upper lip.

Sawyer bit back a laugh and turned his attention back to the boy, who frowned, his small brow furrowed in deep thought.

"Well," he said finally. "I guess we could take turns sitting next to Eeva."

"That's a well thought out plan," Sawyer complimented. "What's your name, my friend?"

"Sol."

Sawyer held out his hand to the boy, and Sol shook it as best he could. "It's very nice to finally meet you, Sol. I'm Sawyer. You know, your mom was pregnant with you the last time I saw her."

"You knew Mom before I was born?"

"We've been friends for a very long time."

Sol looked to his mother, who confirmed with a nod. Then, the boy smiled at him. "Since you're friends with Mom, I'll let you sit next to Eeva for breakfast. But next time, it's my turn."

Sawyer nodded seriously. "Okay. You got it."

CHAPTER 7

The sweet, creamy warmth of her hot chocolate swirled on Evergreen's tongue as she washed down her last bite of omelet. She glanced sideways at Sawyer over the rim of her mug. He didn't notice her looking, but then again, he never had. *It was awfully nice of him to make me cocoa, and he even remembered just how I like it,* she thought. *But why would he do that? I didn't ask him to.*

She smiled into the cup as she downed the last of it. *Don't make it into something it's not,* she told herself. *That's how you got all wrapped up in him before and look what a mess that was. It's just cocoa. He was just being nice, probably making up for teasing me earlier.*

"I have to go to the grocery store today," her dad told everyone at the table. "I've got a lot of cooking ahead of me."

"Could you also go to the craft store if I give you a list?" her mom asked. "I need stuff for the baskets and cotton thread for the candles. I'd go, but we have to get the rest of the rooms ready for everyone. Plus, I have to do laundry and whatnot."

"I can go with you, Dad," Evergreen said. "We can split the effort. I'll go to the craft store, and you can handle the market."

"Thanks, honey. That would be a big help."

"I'd like to go to the craft store, too," Sawyer added. "If you could use an extra pair of hands."

Just as Evergreen opened her mouth to say she was just fine without help, her father agreed.

"I'll stay and help Aunt Ria," Cassandra said.

"Me too," Tara seconded.

"But Mom," Sol complained. "I want to go into town, too." He held out the last word, his voice rising into a whine.

Cassandra glanced at Evergreen, who nodded.

"You can come with me, Sparkler," Evergreen told the boy. "I'm going to need lots of help carrying all the heavy packages."

"I can do that! I can carry the packages," Sol assured.

"Then, it looks like you're just the man for the job."

Twenty minutes later, Cassandra helped Sol put on his boots, coat, hat, and mittens. "You're going to be good for Eeva and Sawyer, right?" she asked him.

"Don't worry," Evergreen assured her cousin. "Sparkler is always good for me."

Cassandra smiled sweetly at her son then kissed him on the cheek. "Okay. I'll see you later then."

He wrapped his arms around his mom's neck. "Bye, Mom. I love you."

"I love you too, sweetheart."

Then, Sol took Evergreen's hand.

"Make sure Muir stays out of trouble, will you?" Evergreen

asked her cousin.

Cassandra nodded, and Evergreen and Sol headed into the cold winter morning.

"All good?" Evergreen asked as they approached her dad's car.

"Yep, all done," Sawyer answered, standing up from securing Sol's car seat. "You ready, my friend?" he asked, turning his attention to the boy.

Sol nodded and climbed into his car seat. Sawyer went about buckling him in as Evergreen went around to sit beside him.

"Ready?" her dad asked, buckling his seatbelt and looking around to make sure everyone else had done the same.

The rest answered in the affirmative.

They made their way toward town. "Did your mom give you the list?" her dad asked as he drove slowly down the snow-lined road.

"Yeah, she said you guys are donating to the women's and children's shelter this year."

"She found out they're running low on supplies."

Evergreen nodded, but she didn't know if he saw her.

"So, Sawyer," her dad started, "I hear you're working at an animal rehabilitation center."

"Yes, I care for the animals and give tours, lead nature hikes, and teach kids about the wildlife when they visit on field trips."

"That sounds right up your alley. You always were good with animals," Wes answered.

"Yeah, it's really rewarding, especially when we get to release them back into the wild. It makes all that patience nursing them back to health worth it."

"You seem like you're enjoying it," Wes said.

"I am," Sawyer agreed, the smile apparent in his voice.

A warmth spread through Evergreen's chest. *He's happy,* she thought. *I can hear it. He found something he loves to do. I'm glad.* And she knew it was true, even as she ignored the tinge of sadness in her stomach.

"Eeva is looking for jobs at the moment. Any luck yet, honey?"

Evergreen sighed. "Not yet."

"Maybe you could send Sawyer your résumé. He's done the whole job search thing before. Maybe he could give you some tips," her dad suggested.

"N—"

"I'd be happy to," Sawyer said, cutting off her objection. "Go ahead and send it to me. Do you…still have my email address?"

Do I still have your email? she thought. *Yeah, I still have it. Just like I still have your phone number, and we're still technically friends on social media.*

Her heart squeezed at the memory of all those checked boxes in the photo gallery of her phone disappearing into a cloud drive folder called Vault so she'd never have to accidentally see any of the pictures of animals or interesting looking trees he'd sent her. Unfollowing him on social media had been even worse. *He has no idea just how hard it was for me to let him go, just how much it tore me apart to recognize all his fleeting glances and sweet gestures for what they really were: warm, kind, and colored with the heart-rending torment of a friendship that fell too short,* she thought.

"Yeah," she murmured. "I still have it."

CHAPTER 8

"I'll pick you up in two hours," Wes said as Sawyer helped Sol from his car seat.

"Okay, Dad," Eeva acknowledged. She pulled her white cane from her bag as he drove away. She unwrapped the elastic and let the sections snap into place.

"I didn't know you could get them in different colors," Sawyer said, nodding to the purple handle and tip of her cane.

"Yeah, companies are finally catching on to just because you're blind, doesn't mean you don't want to look good."

"Eeva, why do you only carry your cane sometimes?" Sol asked. "Don't you need it all the time?"

"You're probably right, Sparkler. If I was smart like you, I'd carry it all the time. But when I'm in a place that I know really well, like at home, I don't really need it. And sometimes, like when I have a lot to carry, I just don't use it. But when I'm in a place where I can easily trip or bump into things or when there are a lot of people who have to know that I don't see them very well, then I try to carry it."

Sol frowned. "I don't want you to get hurt. You should carry it all the time."

Eeva smiled down at the boy. "You're probably right," she said again. "All right. Let's do this. You ready, Sparkler?"

"Ready!" Sol agreed, squeezing Sawyer's hand as they began walking toward the entrance.

The steady clanging from a corner Santa's bell sounded muffled by the insulating snow.

Sol frowned as he watched the man and his red bucket.

"What is it, my friend?" Sawyer asked him. "Why are you giving Santa that look?"

Sol turned his big, brown eyes to Sawyer. "My teacher was reading a book about Santa, and some kids in my class laughed at me when I didn't know the story."

Eeva met Sawyer's gaze, her brow puckered with uncertainty.

"Did your mom tell you about him?" Eeva asked the boy.

Sol frowned. "She told me he was a giving spirit. But I didn't know about any of the other stuff. I didn't know he had flying deer or that he came down the chimney."

Now inside the automatic doors of the craft store, Sawyer knelt down in front of the child. "Storytelling is a big part of how we celebrate Yule. Why don't we ask your mom to tell us the story of Santa tonight?"

"Okay," Sol agreed as if all his concerns had been addressed.

Sawyer helped Sol take off his mittens and hat and unzipped his coat. Then, he stood and looked at Eeva.

Her eyes were warm as she smiled softly at them. Sawyer's

heart jumped in his chest. He'd thought she would never look at him that way again with the reception he'd received.

"I've missed that," he murmured.

Eeva frowned. "Missed what?" she asked.

"Your smile."

Her cheeks flushed, and she averted her eyes.

He smiled. *And I've missed that*, he thought.

"Let's get this done before the old ladies beat us to the good yarn."

"Lead the way." Sawyer swept his hand before them.

She turned to Sol. "Do you want to sit in the cart or walk?"

"I want to walk."

"All right. Then you better stay near Sawyer or me."

Warmth spread through Sawyer as his name left her lips. Yes, she may be different from the Eeva he knew before, but it was clear she still had an effect on him. His skin tingled with the renewed desire to have her eyes only on him, to have her voice whisper only his name.

"I will," Sol promised.

"Will you push the cart?" Eeva asked, turning her attention to Sawyer.

He smiled. "Whatever you need," he promised, his voice thick with implication.

Her cheeks colored again, and her eyebrows crinkled. His grin widened.

She cleared her throat. "Um, okay. Thanks." Then, she turned and led them to the back of the store.

Three full aisles of yarn stood imposingly before them.

Eeva stared down at her list. "Okay, mom wants some

worsted weight wool or alpaca and some skeins of cotton as well."

"What is she making?" Sawyer asked.

"Hats and mittens with the wool, and washcloths with the cotton," she answered. "All right, Sparkler. Let's find what we need. What colors do you like?"

The trio spent the next half hour picking out yarn.

"What else?" Sawyer asked.

Eeva consulted her list. "Looks like baskets to put all the gifts for the shelter in."

Picking the baskets didn't take nearly as long as it had with the yarn. But then, they had to go all the way back to the yarn aisle because they'd forgotten the cotton thread for the candles. Next, they picked out fabric to wrap the soap in. They chose a light blue with snowflakes.

They still had time once they'd gotten everything on the list.

"Do you want to look around a little, Sparkler? Maybe we could find a craft for you."

The boy agreed. "I want to make something for Mom to give to her at Yule."

"Okay. Is there anything special you want to make her?" Eeva asked him.

Sol's brow crinkled in thought. "Something that has to do with the sun."

Eeva smiled. "That's a very appropriate Yule gift. Hmm, how about a sun catcher?"

Sol pursed his lips. "You're teasing me, Eeva. You can't catch the sun."

"Always so skeptical, my little Sparkler. A sun catcher is

something you put in the window. When the sunlight hits it, it lights up, shining rainbows of color all over the room."

Sol's eyes sparkled. "That. I want to make that."

Eeva smirked. "Okay, let's make that."

For Sol's special project, they got clear acrylic discs, each with a hole drilled into it. They also found clear quilting thread, glue, and colored glass dragon tears.

Eeva looked at her cell phone as they put the last of the stuff in the cart. "I think that about does it. Unless you need anything?" she asked, turning her questioning gaze on Sawyer.

"Nope. I'm good."

"Let's head toward the checkout then. Dad should be here soon."

They got into a rather long line of elderly ladies, quite a few of whom indeed had yarn. Eeva gave Sawyer a significant look that said, "I told you so."

When it was their turn, the smiling cashier rang them up, and Eeva paid for the purchases as Sawyer helped Sol put his winter things back on.

"Your receipt is in the bag," the cashier told Eeva.

"Great. Thanks. Happy holidays," Eeva responded, reaching for the cloth bags they'd brought with them.

The cashier frowned. "We say merry Christmas here," she corrected forcefully.

Eeva froze, her face going a bit pale.

Sawyer stood from helping Sol and smiled brightly at the cashier. "Thank you so much for your well wishes. And let me also wish you a very happy Yule. May the gods and goddesses of darkness and light guide you on your journey to enlightenment."

The cashier's mouth hung open, and her eyes bulged.

Sawyer reached out and took their purchases from the counter with one hand; he gently placed his other on Eeva's back.

She glanced over at him, and he smiled.

"Ready?" he asked cheerfully.

Eeva nodded.

Sol took Eeva's hand, and the trio left the store as Sawyer flashed one more smile at the glaring cashier.

CHAPTER 9

Though Evergreen could not feel the warmth of Sawyer's hand on her back through her winter coat, the gentle pressure was reassuring nonetheless.

Sawyer's eyes swept the parking lot. "It doesn't look like he's here yet," he said.

"It shouldn't be too long," Evergreen answered. "Let's just have a seat over there." She gestured toward a bench some twenty feet from the store's entrance.

"Hey, I was supposed to carry the bags!" Sol protested as they started toward the seat.

"Oh, that's right. I'm sorry, my friend." Sawyer handed Sol the lightest bag. "Hold on tight. We don't want to lose anything."

Reaching the bench, Sol stared at it as he tried to work out how he would sit on the higher seat without dropping the bag.

"Why don't I take that, and I can give it back once you're comfortably seated?" Sawyer suggested to the boy.

He nodded, holding the bag out to Sawyer. Then, he climbed into the middle of the bench and demanded it back. Sawyer obliged.

Evergreen and Sawyer took seats on either side of the child.

Staring out at the parking lot, surrounded by massive mounds of plowed snow, Evergreen snickered to herself. She could see Sawyer turn to her from the corner of her eye, and she looked at him.

"That cashier certainly didn't see that coming," she said with a chuckle.

Sawyer's voice was warm. "I'm sorry if I stole your thunder. You looked as though you could use an assist. I hope she didn't upset you too much."

Evergreen shook her head. "Nah, I was just surprised. You hang around with other Pagans too long, and you sort of forget just how few of us there are compared to everyone else. Plus, you know, you never expect someone to be so militant about something nice like happy holidays."

"You don't have campus crusaders at your university?"

Evergreen nodded. "Of course we do. But they don't know when our student group meets. And we know when to expect them. We know they'll show up to protest Pagan Pride Day and anything we actively advertise, so we're ready to put on our thicker skins and ignore them." She shrugged. "But I don't know. I guess I just wasn't ready this time."

Sawyer nodded, his silence heavy with thought and maybe a twinge of sadness. Evergreen frowned. She didn't like that feeling coming from him, and she mentally kicked herself for bringing up such topics.

"I wish people could leave us to be ourselves," he murmured. "I wish we didn't have to hide so much, that we didn't have to fight so much." He met her eyes. "I wish I could make it so you never had to be afraid to be your whole self, Eeva, that Sol could grow up and never learn what it means to keep a part of himself hidden."

Evergreen's chest ached at his words, and she had the urge to go back and give that cashier a piece of her mind. *How dare she make Sawyer feel this way!* But she knew it wouldn't help even if she did. She sighed and shook her head. "This is the path we've chosen," she said. "Just because it's hard doesn't mean we should give up. Maybe one day people will be more tolerant. Maybe by the time Sol is our age he can openly be himself without fear of retribution. In any case, that's what we fight for. Isn't it? And we will keep fighting, even if that day never comes."

Sawyer nodded. "But it would be nice if we didn't have to fight."

Evergreen smiled at his soft-heartedness. "For how many centuries have we been fighting? At least we're still around. Right? I mean, they haven't stamped us out completely no matter how hard they tried. The old ways still survive, and I don't think they're going anywhere. There will always be those who hear the call of this path and follow it."

"You've always had the heart of a warrior," Sawyer murmured, his tone distant but smiling. "I remember that time you got detention for standing up in assembly and proclaiming that forcing us all to bow our heads and pray violated our rights."

Evergreen grinned at the memory. "And you've always been the peacekeeper. If I recall, you went to the principal's office and requested that if they insisted on praying that they should have a moment of silence as opposed to a Christian prayer so all students of different faiths may pray or abstain as they wish."

Sawyer smiled warmly, and Evergreen felt that hint of sadness dissipate. "You inspired me. You always did."

A shiver ran through Evergreen as her cheeks heated. She averted her eyes, looking back out toward the parking lot. "Yeah, well. That was a long time ago. A lot has changed since then."

"So you aren't still fired up to take on the establishment every chance you get?" he asked, his voice thick with mock astonishment.

"I've learned to pick my battles," she answered. *I've learned to be more like you,* she thought.

"When is Uncle Wes coming?" Sol asked. "I'm hungry."

Evergreen squinted down the street in search of her father's car. There was no sign of it yet.

"You are? Well, then it's a good thing I just so happen to have this chocolate chip granola bar in my pocket," Sawyer said, taking the snack from his jacket and shaking it at the boy.

"Ooo! Can I have it?"

"Mmmm, I don't know. It looks awfully delicious. Do you know the magic word?"

"Pleeeeaase!" Sol begged.

"Okay," Sawyer agreed. "Let me open it for you."

Evergreen watched the exchange, warmth spreading through her chest. "You really are good with him," she murmured to herself, smiling softly.

She was relieved Sawyer hadn't heard her over Sol's squeals of delight. Because as he looked up and met her gaze again, her heart skipped a beat, and an old familiar feeling pooled in her stomach. *No,* she thought, crushing the feeling down. *Not this time.*

CHAPTER 10

*W*as that smile for me or Sol? Sawyer wondered as they all rode back to the retreat center. Wes was telling them about how he'd gotten stuff to make suet for the birds tomorrow, but Sawyer wasn't really listening. He looked at Eeva out of the corner of his eye. She stared out the window, her thoughts her own.

He pictured the soft curve of her lips as she smiled after he'd given Sol the granola bar. His heartbeat echoed the pounding of fifteen minutes before. *It was for me. Wasn't it?* he thought. *She smiled when we talked about the past. She smiled, and I was right back to what it felt like back then. No. That's not true.* He knew himself too well to believe it was the same. When she'd smiled at him this time, he'd felt his heartbeat in his neck and fingertips. This wasn't the crush of a shy schoolboy. *This time it's worse.* It wasn't the simple attraction he'd felt for others. This was different. *This is Eeva. There's no going back after this.*

Sawyer took a deep breath and let it out slowly. *I may be*

feeling like this, but that doesn't mean Eeva is, he thought. *She doesn't even know me anymore. I can't let this time be like the last time. I have to tell her this time for sure. And if she doesn't feel the same...* His chest squeezed painfully. *Well, at least then I'll know.*

Once they arrived back at the center, Wes and Sawyer carried in the bags, and Eeva helped Sol from his car seat and ushered him into the house. They put the bags on the dining room table where Ria, Tara, and Cassandra were taking a break.

"How was your mission?" Ria asked her husband.

Wes nodded. "I think we got everything," he answered before giving her a kiss. "And yours?"

She shrugged. "We got a load of laundry done and a few of the rooms cleaned. We can finish the rest tomorrow. Everything should be ready by the time everyone else arrives."

As Sol cuddled happily on his mother's lap, Tara tilted her head at Sawyer.

"What is it, Sawyer? You're wearing your stressed face," his mother said.

He shook his head. "Nothing, Mom. I'm fine. I'm just going to go outside and ground myself a bit."

Sawyer left the dining room and went out the sliding glass door of the common room. The patio had been cleared of snow, but the lawn chairs that usually sat around the stone fire ring had been put away for the winter. Sawyer shuffled to the edge of the patio and stared into the woods behind the house, the dirt path showing in patches below the tree branches, thick with snow.

He breathed deep the freezing air, the chill tickling his nostrils and making him feel like he had to sneeze.

The sliding door opened and shut behind him, and his mom shuffled up beside him. He glanced over at her.

"Mom, what are you doing out here? You're going to get cold with just a blanket," he chided.

She smiled at his concern. "Oh, I won't be out here for long."

She stood by him in companionable silence, staring at the same path through the woods. "Eeva told us what happened with the cashier at the craft store. Is that what has you upset?" she asked finally.

He shook his head. "No, I'm not upset. I'm… Mom, do ever wish you'd never married Dad? I mean, with how everything turned out."

"No. Even though our marriage ended in divorce, even if I'm not in love with your father anymore, I will always be grateful to him. He gave me the greatest gift in life. Without him, I never would have had you. And being a mother… It's what I was meant to do."

Sawyer smiled softly to himself. "You are pretty awesome at it."

"I know, right?" she said in a teasing tone. "So let me do my thing." She cleared her throat formally. "What's bothering you, son?"

Sawyer chuckled before letting his smile slip. He sighed. "It's worse this time, Mom. I can already tell. It's like while I was away from her I forgot what it was like to be in her presence, like I forgot how to breathe. And then I see her and she smiles, and it all comes rushing in like crushing water from a burst dam. I feel…desperate. Like I have to take one more deep breath before sinking below the surface."

"And the water is…?"

"It's the feeling I know is coming if I mess this up again."

"What makes you so sure you're going to mess it up?"

Sawyer shrugged. "I'm not. I'm just afraid I will. I did before. And she…she wasn't exactly pleased to see me."

His mother rubbed slow circles on his back. "You have such a good and kind heart, Sawyer. Why don't you think she will see that?"

"Even if she does, that doesn't mean she'll choose me. She didn't before."

"Well, you didn't tell her how you felt before either. And neither of you are the same as you were before. You can't control whether she chooses you or not. You can only control how you act not how she reacts. You already know what you need to do. If you hadn't already decided to be honest with her, you wouldn't be this anxious. I know you're scared. But courage is doing what's hard despite that fear, right?"

"You're right."

"Aren't I always?" his mom said with a grin. She stepped in front of him, placing her chilled hands on either side of his face. "You are beautiful, my boy. And I know you will find someone worthy of you. I feel it."

"Is this the mom or the witch talking?"

"Both."

The threatening torrent retreated a little at his mother's assurances.

"Okay, but let's get inside. It's freezing out here," she urged.

He chuckled. "I'll make you some tea," he promised as they headed back toward the lodge.

CHAPTER 11

*E*vergreen sat at the dining room table, her tablet propped up before her in its detachable keyboard. Everyone else had gone about their after-lunch business.

Evergreen bit her lip as her heart squeezed in anxiety. The little envelope icon on her screen showed that she had one unread email. She inhaled deeply and held it, tapping on the icon with her fingertip.

Her eyes scanned the form letter. *We regret to inform you...* she knew the rest. She let the breath go, her stomach dropping as though the air had been holding it up. She buried her face in her crossed arms on the table before her, pushing the tablet away with her elbows.

"Are you going to send me your résumé?" Sawyer asked, his voice coming from the doorway in front of her.

She rolled her head to the side, not bothering to even lift it. "Why does it matter? It's not like it's going to help. No one wants to hire me anyway," she said miserably.

His voice grew louder as he came closer. "It's tough out there, but I've never known you to give up so easily. Me giving it the once over certainly won't hurt. Will it?"

She was too despondent to argue with him. "Do what you want. It's on the home screen." She slid the tablet farther from her on the table. She didn't look up but heard him pull it toward him as he sat beside her.

He didn't speak again for a while, and she just used the silence to wallow, her slow breaths loud in her ears as she breathed into the space created by her folded arms.

"Can I ask you something?" he said finally.

"What?" She still didn't look up.

"You're GPA is amazing. You're probably going to graduate with honors. You've done multiple internships, and you even did work-study in your university library archives. But what do you want to do when you graduate? What sort of jobs are you applying for?"

Evergreen slowly raised her head and rested her chin in her hands. "What I want and what I'm qualified for are two different things," she said. "I've been applying for pretty much any job that will take a B.A. in history."

Sawyer frowned. "What do you *want* to do?"

Evergreen sighed. "It doesn't matter. I would have to go to school for a lot longer. I'm already way too far in debt with student loans as it is. I can't go for a higher degree."

His voice was tinged with concern. "You didn't get any scholarships?"

"I got a few small ones. But I went out of state my first year, and there weren't many scholarships for transfer students."

"Yeah," he agreed. "But say you can do whatever you want. What would it be?"

There was a heavy pause before she answered. "If I didn't have to worry about paying for school, I'd go on to get my PhD and become a museum curator."

"Okay, but not everyone at a museum needs a PhD, right? Couldn't you get an entry level position and get a higher degree part time?"

"What do you think I've been trying to do?" she snapped.

"Well, you didn't list that among the things you've been trying," Sawyer said softly, and Evergreen felt bad for having taken her frustration out on him.

"I'm sorry." She sighed. "I'm just really worried. I only have one semester left, and six months later, they're going to come after me for these student loans."

"I understand," he said. "Let me do some research, okay? I will get back to you."

"Thanks," she murmured.

"Have you pulled some cards for advice?" he asked.

Evergreen dropped her head in a slow nod. "Yeah, but I think I'm too emotionally charged to read myself properly on this one. So I'm not getting a clear feel from them."

"Have you had anyone else read you?"

She shook her head. "No, most of the people in the Pagan Student Association at my school have been super busy and stressed about their own stuff. I don't want to bother them."

"I could cast some runes for you if you want."

Evergreen met Sawyer's eyes. It took a lot of concentration for her to maintain eye contact what with her eyes' natural tendency to wander. But she stared at him. *Why? Why does he want to help?* she wondered. *He hasn't been involved with anything in my life for almost five years. He left for college and dropped off the face of the Earth. No texts, calls, messages, nothing. Now he wants to cast runes on my behalf?*

Whatever she thought she'd find in his gaze, she didn't. There was just Sawyer, his expression open and friendly, quite unlike the reserved introvert she remembered, unlike the boy full of shy kindness.

"You're different," she stated.

He didn't look away from her gaze. "I am," he agreed. "But not where it counts."

Evergreen tilted her head at this assertion. *What does that mean?* she wondered.

"Eeva," Sawyer started, his tone gentle but strong. "I know we were never very…close. I mean, we were around each other a lot, but we didn't much confide in each other. Still, I always thought of us as friends. Didn't you?"

"Friends…" Evergreen murmured. The word left a bitter taste in her mouth, and her heart sank in a feeling she recognized all too well despite the lapsed time. "Yeah," she agreed softly.

"I'm sorry if you thought I was teasing you this morning. I really didn't mean to make you feel that way. It's been so long since we've seen each other. I'd like it if we could get along, catch up and everything. Maybe we could get to know each other again?"

Evergreen could hear the fragile hope in his tone, and she couldn't bring herself to crush it. "Sure, Sawyer. I'd like that," she said.

And as Sawyer smiled, his furrowed brow smoothing out in

relief at her answer, Evergreen repeated to herself not to let him in. She could be polite, cordial even, but she could not afford to let him back into her heart. *We won't be here that long,* she thought. *I can manage until we go our separate ways again.*

CHAPTER 12

Sawyer rose from the table. "Let's go," he said.

Eeva's eyebrows scrunched together. "What?"

"I'm going to pull some runes for you. You never know, there could be good news, advice even."

Eeva bit her lip indecisively.

"Come on," he urged gently. "What's it going to hurt?"

With a heavy sigh, Eeva rose from the table. Sawyer beamed a smile.

"My runes are in my bag. The meditation room should be quiet enough for a runecast."

He led the way, and she followed. The moment they crossed the threshold to the meditation room, the temperature dropped perceptively.

"Oof, it's cold in here," Eeva said. "I'm going to set up the heater."

As she executed her task, Sawyer went to his suitcase and pulled out a red suede, drawstring bag. Then, he settled cross-legged in the middle of the room. After pulling a white, cotton cloth from the bag, he spread it out on the floor before him. Eeva sat opposite him.

"It's been a while since I've studied runes," she admitted.

"Don't worry. I'll explain all the meanings as we go. Ready?" Sawyer looked up, meeting Eeva's eyes.

She nodded.

"First let's take a few cleansing breaths to center ourselves."

Sawyer closed his eyes and breathed slowly in through his nose and out through his mouth. As he breathed deep again, his muscles relaxed, and his heart slowed. On the third breath, goosebumps raised on his arms, and he shivered once. He was ready. In his mind's eye, Sawyer visualized a bright green glow emanating from his chest and engulfing him and Eeva in an orb of light. With another deep breath, he opened his eyes and met Eeva's steady gaze.

Holding the bag above the white cloth, Sawyer shook it vigorously a few times. "Pick three," he instructed.

Eeva reached into the bag he offered and laid out her choices on the cloth between them. Sawyer put the bag aside and leaned forward.

"Past, present, future," he said, pointing to each of the runes in turn. "In the past position, you have Ansuz, Odin's rune. Ansuz is a rune that represents communication. But here it's reversed. It could mean that you have received unwanted messages, like your rejection letters. Or it could symbolize miscommunication or misunderstood messages."

Sawyer looked up and met Eeva's eyes. She nodded her understanding.

"In the present, you have Kenaz, the torch. This is a rune of illumination and clarity. It is sudden enlightenment and understanding. In regards to your previous rune, I'd say that whatever misunderstanding happened in the past, it will be cleared up. It can also sometimes mean an offer, like a job. In any case, this is your present. So, if it hasn't happened already, it's going to happen very soon."

"And the future?" Eeva asked, pointing to the last rune she had laid out.

"Wunjo." Sawyer looked up from the runes, meeting Eeva's gaze once more. "Joy," he said simply.

Light crept into Eeva's eyes. "Really?" she asked, her voice only just above a whisper.

Sawyer nodded.

Eeva placed a palm on her chest and sighed, closing her eyes as she did so. "Thank the gods."

"You're going to be just fine, Eeva," Sawyer reassured.

She met his gaze and smiled softly. "Thank you, Sawyer."

His heart thumped hard in his chest. That smile, that tender look in her eyes, that was for him. He knew that was for him.

"You're welcome," he whispered, unable to get enough air to say it properly.

"Did you make these?" Eeva asked, staring down at the runes.

Sawyer nodded. "Yes, I made them from a fallen branch of ash. I sawed it into discs and used a wood burner to carve the runes into them."

"They're beautiful," she said, reaching out and caressing Wunjo.

Sawyer's chest swelled. "Thank you," he murmured.

"You always were good with your hands," Eeva said. "You

even built all the sets for the drama club, didn't you? I remember the one you built for the mermaid's lagoon when we did *Peter Pan*. It was really good."

She noticed that? Sawyer thought. *I mean, she obviously knew I was set crew, but I didn't think she paid that close attention.*

"Thanks," he said. "I had to make sure I did a good job on that one. You were one of the mermaids. I didn't want to ruin your scene."

"Oh man, those mermaid outfits were awful! I could barely walk in that tail."

The image of Eeva in a seashell bikini top and shimmering blue mermaid tail rose in Sawyer's mind.

"Well, it looked good," he said honestly.

Eeva's sharp eyes flicked to his face. "Maybe," she said.

Sawyer remembered how she had fawned over Sean Ferguson. And Sean had loved every second of it. Sawyer had even overheard him during dress rehearsal talking about what he'd like to do to her with the actor who had played Captain Hook. *Would Eeva have been into a guy like that?* he wondered. *She never had a boyfriend in high school, so she must not have been. Sean didn't seem the type to be shy about his interest.* Sawyer had known that her giggles and squeals at Sean on stage were only part of the script, but that hadn't stopped his chest from hurting at the sight.

"You were a pretty convincing actress," he said.

"You think so? I don't know. I was never very good at nuanced parts. That's why I always tried out for the outrageous characters."

"Did you…stay in contact with any of the people from drama club?" he asked, trying to sound offhand. He didn't remember seeing any posts on her social media about hanging out with them, but that didn't mean it didn't happen. He tried to remember the names of the guys she had listed on her page as being in a relationship with. Tyler, Dean, and Marty, though Marty hadn't lasted more than a few weeks.

Eeva frowned. "Not really. I didn't really stay in contact with anyone from high school. I was ready to move on with my life. Start fresh."

Sawyer's heart squeezed, and his gaze dropped with his stomach. *That includes you, Sawyer,* he thought, finishing the rest of her unsaid statement.

"A-and you?" she asked.

Sawyer looked up at her.

"Do you still talk to people from high school?" Her voice was steady and unconcerned, but her eyebrows were bunched together as if his answer mattered very much to her.

"Not really. I get the odd message on social media every now and then, but everyone is doing their own thing. Plus, I went pretty far away for college."

Eeva nodded slowly.

"But I'm glad to be here now," he added. "Eeva, I never intended—"

"Here you two are," Cassandra interrupted, opening the door to the meditation room. Her eyes found the runes on the floor between them. "Oh, am I interrupting a reading?" She sucked in air through her teeth. "Sorry," she whispered, dipping her head.

"Don't worry. We were already finished," Eeva said.

"Oh, okay. Good. Well, dinner is ready," Cassandra informed.

Eeva rose from the floor. "Okay. I'm coming." Then, she left.

Cassandra tilted her head at Sawyer in a question.

"Yeah, me too. Let me just clean these up first."

Sawyer picked up the three runes from the white cloth and dropped them into their bag. As he folded the cloth, Cassandra pointed to the floor beside him.

"You dropped one," she told him. Then, she made her exit as well.

"Huh, it must have jumped out while I was shaking the bag," Sawyer muttered to the empty room.

Flipping the rune over in his hand, his breath caught in his throat as an X burned into the wood clarified the runecast.

"Gebo," he whispered. "Gift. The rune of union and partnership… The herald of love."

CHAPTER 13

*E*vergreen slipped another stitch from the left needle to the right. It had been a while since she'd knit. And though it came back to her without much effort, she'd decided to start small with a washcloth rather than daring the double pointed needles for a hat or mittens.

Ria and Tara sat on either side of her on the couch, her mother just pulling the top of a knitted hat tight as Tara made a topper pom. Seated on the floor at the coffee table, Sawyer patiently took the finished works and weaved the ends in with a yarn needle. Beside him, Sol colored in his Little Pagans coloring book, his fist clutching a green crayon.

On the floor, Wes had laid out the blue fabric they had gotten at the craft store. He was attempting to cut it into small, even squares, but Muir and Larkspur were giving him trouble by laying on it in turns.

"Tea break," Cassandra announced, entering the living room

with a tea service tray. Sawyer moved the projects from the coffee table so she had somewhere to place the tray.

"Smells good," Evergreen said, placing her knitting beside her and moving her sore wrists in slow circles.

Cassandra poured each of the adults a cup before offering the cream and sugar. Lastly, she sat beside Sol on the floor, placing a cup of milk before him.

"Mom," Sol started, calling for Cassandra's attention with a very serious tone.

"Sol," Cassandra acknowledged, turning to him with an equally serious voice.

"Sawyer told me I should ask you about Santa," Sol said.

Cassandra turned to Sawyer, but she was too far away for Evergreen to see her expression.

"We saw Santa outside the craft store today, and Sol said the kids at school were teasing him because he didn't know some of the stories about him," Evergreen explained.

"Sol, honey, why didn't you tell me about the kids at school?" his mother asked, concerned.

"You have a lot to worry about," Sol murmured. "I didn't want to bother you."

Cassandra reached out and stroked her son's hair. "Sol, you could never be a bother to me. I always want you to tell me your problems. It makes me sad when you don't confide in me, sweetheart."

"I don't want to make you sad, Mama. I will tell you from now on. I promise," Sol vowed.

"Good. So, you want to know more about Santa?"

The boy nodded.

"Do you remember a few years ago when you saw Santa at

the mall, and you asked about him?"

"Yes, you told me he was a giving spirit."

Cassandra smiled. "That's right. Santa is very special. He is a spirit of kindness and generosity, and he is particularly invoked this time of year. So, people give each other gifts in his name or perform acts of kindness. Just like what we're doing now. We're making gift baskets for the women and children at the shelter. That's the kind thing to do when they need help." She explained the same way they had been taught as children.

"But what about the flying deer?"

"Every spirit has a backstory. You know that. Some chariots are pulled by cats, some peacocks, some horses. Santa's is pulled by reindeer."

"My friends said that only good kids get toys from Santa," Sol said.

"Well that's not true at all. You know that toys cost money. What if a family doesn't have enough money to get their children presents? That doesn't mean that poor children are bad. Does it?" Cassandra asked.

"No," Sol agreed, following her logic. "But…" He hesitated, his voice uncertain as he worked through his thoughts. "But we should be kind to everyone, right? I want to invoke Santa, too. I'm going to color pictures and put them in the baskets. Do you think they would like that?"

Cassandra kissed her son's head. "I think that gifts that come from the heart are the best kind, and you have a very big heart, my boy."

Sol turned back toward his coloring book. "I have to hurry," he told his mom. "I don't have a lot of time before Yule."

Evergreen sniffed hard, wiping her eyes on her long sleeve.

Cassandra is doing such a good job raising Sparkler, she thought. Then, she leaned over on her mom, resting her head on Ria's shoulder. Ria wrapped an arm around Evergreen and kissed her temple. Evergreen wasn't really the touchy-feely sort. She liked to maintain her personal space. But when she wanted physical contact, she needed it like a wound that needs pressure.

It wasn't long after that Cassandra told Sol it was time for bed. He complained, of course, saying he had a lot of work to do for the people at the shelter.

"You have enough time to work on your presents tomorrow," Cassandra assured.

"Can I say goodnight first?"

Cassandra nodded.

Sol crossed the room to Wes and gave him a hug. Then, he hugged Sawyer, then Tara, then Evergreen, and finally Ria. He went back to Wes and hugged him again. When he returned to Sawyer for another hug, Sawyer chuckled at the boy, the sound rich and sweet.

"That's enough," Cassandra said, her voice barely holding in a laugh. "You'll see everyone tomorrow."

"Just one more," Sol negotiated.

"Okay."

Sol gave another hug to Tara, Ria, and Evergreen.

"Goodnight, Sparkler," Evergreen murmured as the boy's head rested on her chest. "Sweet dreams."

"Goodnight, Eeva. I hope you have good dreams, too."

As Cassandra led her son upstairs, quiet laughter traveled through those he'd left behind.

It wasn't long until Evergreen's eyes were heavy, and her hands slowed in her knitting.

"Why don't you go up to bed, sweetheart?" Ria suggested as Evergreen leaned more heavily against her.

"I'm not tired," Evergreen lied.

"We all know you're not a night person," her father pointed out. "You never have been."

"You barely made it through our esbat rituals," Tara agreed.

"I'm an adult now. I've changed," Evergreen argued.

"There's nothing wrong with being a morning person, Eeva," Sawyer said. "They say it's much healthier actually."

Evergreen frowned, knowing she couldn't really make a good case. "I think I'm going to go to bed," she said as if it was her idea all along.

"Goodnight," Sawyer said, his voice sounding suspiciously like he was smirking.

CHAPTER 14

When Sawyer entered the common room the next morning, he found Eeva sitting cross-legged on the floor, leaning her elbows on the table with the television set, her face a foot and a half from the screen. Muir lay curled up in her lap, sleeping. She glanced over at him only long enough to see who had entered.

"Good morning," he mumbled, his voice still graveled from sleep.

"Morning," she responded automatically, not taking her eyes from the screen. "No one else is up yet. Feel free to make yourself some coffee."

"Can I get you anything while I'm in the kitchen?" he offered.

"No, I'm good. Thanks."

Sawyer went to the kitchen and started the coffee pot, breathing deep as he scooped the grounds into the filter basket.

With a fresh cup in his hand, he returned to the living room and placed his mug on the table.

Eeva glanced over her shoulder as he sat on the couch. "Do you need me to move?" she asked. "Can you see around me?"

"You're fine. I can see," he answered.

Sawyer watched as Margaret Sullavan insulted Jimmy Stewart without mercy, a copy of Tolstoy and a red carnation on the café table between them.

Sawyer smiled to himself. He'd seen the film many times before, every Yule since he was fourteen, since his mother joined the coven. It was Eeva's favorite holiday movie.

"You're not still calling this a holiday movie. Are you?" he teased.

"If *Die Hard* counts as a holiday movie then so does this," she countered primly.

He agreed with her, but he took a little pleasure in getting under her skin. "Whatever you say."

She shushed him as if she didn't know what was going to happen. "Just because you don't want to watch doesn't mean I don't."

He hadn't said he didn't want to watch it. *I wonder what she'd say if she knew I've watched it every year since I saw her last,* he thought. *She probably wouldn't believe me.*

As the movie continued on, Sawyer paid little attention to it. He was too busy watching Eeva's reactions. Her eyes sparkled with laughter at William Tracy's antics, and she giggled freely. So long had it been since he'd seen such carefree joy in her. His chest warmed at the sight. *Could I ever be a source of easy happiness for her?* he wondered.

Eeva grinned, her cheeks pink with restrained delight as

Jimmy Stewart finally put the red carnation in his buttonhole. She laughed as he pulled up his pant legs and sighed contentedly as he bent down to kiss the heroine.

"Kissing seems so different in old movies. Don't you think?" she commented as the screen declared that it was the end. "I don't know. Somehow, it's more passionate in a way. Less sexual but more passionate. I wonder why it feels that way."

Sawyer tilted his head in thought. "I read once that there were rules and conventions back then about how long actors could kiss at a time. I think it was only three seconds. That would mean they would have to pack in all the passion that would later be able to build slowly into just three seconds. Maybe that's why."

Eeva nodded. "That makes sense. Interesting. I wonder what other kinds of rules they had." She pulled out her phone to answer the question for herself.

Sawyer followed her lead, using the time to track down some ideas he had about her job problem.

"Wow, listen to this. There were rules against cursing and certain dance moves. They couldn't show interracial couples. They couldn't even talk about sexual diseases."

"You're surprised?" he asked, looking over his phone at her.

"I mean, yes and no. This code was in effect until 1967, and how can they put restrictions on art? Where is the freedom of speech?"

"Come on, you've been Pagan your whole life. You think there is really freedom of religion and speech in this country?"

Eeva frowned, the light in her eyes dimming a little. "Yeah… you're right," she murmured. "Even if they say there is, it doesn't make it true effectively. I guess I never stop being surprised by it. The narrative is so different from the reality. They fill your head full of promises and high ideals, and so I'm just a little taken aback when I'm faced with how it really is. They tell us that we are the freest country. The land of opportunity. But that really only applies when you're the right gender, the right color, worship the right god, love the right person."

Sawyer didn't like the uncharacteristic hopelessness in her voice. "But it's like you said yesterday. We have to keep fighting. That's just how it is if we want to survive. And maybe, maybe one day we can be as free as they keep telling us we are."

She smiled sadly, curling around the purring cat in her lap. "Maybe," she murmured.

"On a side note, I think I found something that might help you with your career goals."

She tilted her head. "What do you mean?"

"Have you heard of a museum certificate?"

"No."

"It's a certificate that seems to help people break into the museum field. It's only like sixteen credits to get, and you may have some of them already. You might have to go to school for an extra semester, two tops if the classes don't line up right. And it requires an internship. I'm sure the college has museums it partners with so students can complete their requirements. I even found some people on forums saying that their internships landed them full time positions. Some said the museums are paying for them to go on with their studies, too."

"What? Really? I wonder if my university offers it."

Sawyer grinned. "I already looked. It does. Here, I'll text you the link."

CHAPTER 15

Evergreen hadn't realized just how far into hopelessness she had fallen, just how bad her anxiety had gotten until Sawyer had pointed out a direction. She would have to do more research of course. But the knot in her stomach had loosened, and her breathing came easy.

She looked over at Sawyer as he stood beside her at the kitchen island. He was helping Sol measure out the shortening for the suet they were making. Sawyer scooped it into the measuring cup Sol tried to hold steady.

"That's it," Sawyer said with a smile, dumping the contents into a saucepan.

"Now what?" Sol asked.

"Now for the nut butter. We need three-fourths of a cup. Can you tell me what measuring cup we should use?"

Sol hummed, staring at the assembled cups. "That one." He pointed to the smallest.

"That's right! Good job," Sawyer praised. "All right, you got the nut butter?"

Sol took the jar from the counter and tried the lid, his little elbows stuck out to the sides as he grunted. "It won't open," he complained. "I need help."

"No problem, my friend. I got your back." Sawyer took the jar from him and opened it without effort.

Then, he handed it back to Sol, helping him measure out the right amount into the pan.

Evergreen smiled at the pair, her chest warming at their exchange.

"How's your part coming, Eeva?" Sawyer asked. He turned toward her, his amber eyes finding hers.

Her heart jumped, and she could feel the blush raising in her cheeks, telling the tale of her spying. She looked down at the gathered ingredients she still had to assemble into her mixing bowl. "Almost finished," she lied, even though he could clearly see she hadn't put anything in the bowl.

"Okay then," he answered. She could hear the smile in his voice, but she didn't look over to confirm.

"What do we do next?" Sol asked.

"Next, we wash your hands." Sawyer picked up the boy and carried him over to the sink.

Evergreen quickly measured out the birdseed, oats, and cornmeal as the faucet ran behind her.

"I like your pentacle necklace," Sol told Sawyer as the man returned the boy to his step stool.

"Thank you."

"Where did you get it?"

"Nowhere special. Just online."

"Oh. Well it's really nice."

"I tell you what, since you like it, why don't you have it?" Sawyer pulled the black-corded silver pentacle over his head and put it around the child's neck.

Sol looked down at the pendant, which hung to his sternum, then looked up at Sawyer, beaming. "Thank you, Sawyer."

"You're welcome. Hey, can you tell me what the five points of the pentacle represent?"

"Oh sure, that's easy," the boy replied proudly. "Earth, air, fire, water, and spirit."

"You sure are smart. You obviously pay attention to all the things your mama teaches you."

Sawyer held out his fist, and Sol bumped it with his considerably smaller one.

"Okay, let's melt this and add the dry ingredients," Sawyer said, taking the saucepan and the mixing bowl to the stove.

A while later as Evergreen spooned the hot mixture into a silicone ice cube tray, her mother entered the kitchen.

"Hey, would you two mind going into town when you're done? I thought I had enough bottles for the shampoo, but I miscounted. Eeva, you know what kind I use. Sawyer, would you mind driving her?"

"Not at all," Sawyer responded.

"Can I go too, Aunt Ria?" Sol asked.

"Not this time, Sparkler. It's nap time for you."

The boy groaned but didn't argue.

I guess it can't be helped, Evergreen thought. "Sure, Mom," she agreed.

"Great. Thanks," Ria said.

As Evergreen slid into the passenger seat of Sawyer's car,

she became overly aware of how close he was. His presence was heavy and insistent, and she couldn't escape his scent all around her.

"Do you mind if I put on some music?" she murmured.

"Go ahead."

Evergreen pressed the button, and the dulcet tones of Loreena McKennitt emanated from the speakers. She grinned. "Your mom pick this?"

"Hey, I like her too," he defended. Then, he chuckled. "But yeah, she's my mom's favorite. If you want to change it, there are CDs in the center console."

"Let's see what you have," Evergreen said, pulling out the discs more for something to do than to actually change the music. She flipped through. *Blackmore's Night, Celtic Women, Led Zeppelin,* Evergreen read the artists in her mind. *Oh, this was always his favorite,* she thought, pulling the CD from its sleeve. She removed Loreena McKennitt and popped in the new disc, navigating to number four.

As the upbeat melody filled the car, Evergreen glanced at Sawyer. When he smiled over at her, her heart danced with the music of "Tanz mit mir."

"You remembered?"

She lowered her face, suddenly self-conscious that she had brought attention to her past weakness for him. "Well...you know, it was hard to forget. You played it so often. I mean, you even took German in high school to be able to understand their lyrics."

"I did," he agreed. "And I still remember them." He reached forward and turned up the volume, singing loudly, his voice pleasant and energetic.

Evergreen bobbed her head and tapped her foot to the beat, letting the music carry away the awkwardness she'd felt since getting into the car.

Though they didn't have to get very many bottles from the craft store, it took them quite a while as the place was packed with people just picking something up during their lunch breaks. Without any verbal agreement, they avoided the cashier they had the previous day.

As they finally returned to the fresh air and headed for the car, Sawyer said, "Gods, that took forever."

"I know. I'm starving."

"Me too. Hey, do you want to get something to eat? I haven't had Mediterranean Smoothie since I went off to college."

Evergreen hesitated. "I mean, my dad should be making lunch."

"You don't understand," he said seriously. "Now, I have the expectation of Violet Rave in my mouth. It won't go away until it's satisfied. Please, Eeva. I'll buy you lunch," he ended with a plea.

"Pff," Evergreen chuckled. "I mean, I'm not stupid. Who would say no to free lunch?"

"Yes!" Sawyer exclaimed, holding the ending S with a hiss.

"You're going to regret making this offer," she warned. "I'm not shy when it comes to eating."

"It'll be worth it for the Violet Rave."

Mediterranean Smoothie was just starting to calm down after the lunch rush, the few empty tables being wiped down by bussers. After they took a seat, the waitress appeared and handed them their menus.

"Can I get you started with anything to drink?" she asked in a chipper tone.

"I'll have the Violet Rave," Sawyer told her.

Evergreen squinted at the menu.

"You know you'll make yourself go blind holding the menu that close," the waitress joked.

Evergreen took a slow, deep breath. "Too late," she muttered.

The waitress paused for a moment, unsure what she meant.

"I have to hold it this close. I'm legally blind, and I can't read it if I don't," Evergreen said patiently as if the waitress deserved an explanation.

"Oh my god. I'm so sorry," the waitress gasped. "I didn't know. I mean, you don't *look* blind."

Evergreen let that one go. No good would come from explaining to the woman just how rude of a comment that was. Sure, she might understand that blindness could be caused by so many things. But she clearly didn't get that blindness didn't have a *look*. And really, she didn't want to make the woman any more uncomfortable by pointing out that she'd just insulted the entire blind community, especially when she clearly had thought she was giving Evergreen a compliment.

"I'll have a mango smoothie, please," Evergreen said, ignoring the comment altogether.

As the waitress walked away to fill their orders, Evergreen rubbed her eyes, having had to strain them to read the too small print.

"You all right?" Sawyer asked.

"Yeah, fine. Thanks."

"Is there—"

"Oh my goodness, Sawyer Collins. Is that you?"

Sawyer turned as a chic African American woman entered the restaurant.

"Lay-Lay?" his voice raised in confused delight. He rose from his seat and went to hug the woman. "Wow, it has been so long. How are you?"

"Oh, I'm just out here being my fabulous self as always."

"Of course. I wouldn't have expected anything less."

"But look at you all tall and handsome. I see you grew into those lanky arms after all. And you even have a girl with you. Oh, is that Evergreen Pendre?"

"Oh, sorry, yeah."

The pair walked the few steps to the table.

"Eeva, you remember Allaya, right?"

Evergreen dipped her head, forcing a smile as her stomach dropped. *Do I remember your best friend and high school crush? How could I forget?* she thought.

"Of course. I'm glad to see you again, Allaya. How are you doing?"

"Wonderful. Graduated last year and opened an interior design business."

"That's great," Eeva said. "I mean, you designed all the sets for drama club, and you were so good at it."

Allaya smiled. "Thank you."

"Lay-Lay, are you meeting someone here? Do you want to join us for lunch?" Sawyer asked. "You don't mind. Right, Eeva?"

"Of course not. Please, join us." Evergreen was quite impressed with her pleasant and convincing tone.

"Thank you," Allaya said again, taking the chair beside Sawyer.

"I'll be right back. I have to go to the bathroom," Evergreen told them. "If the waitress comes back, please tell her I want a chicken gyro pita."

"No problem," Sawyer confirmed.

Get your shit together, Evergreen thought. *Allaya has always been nice to you. And you don't even like Sawyer anymore, so there's no need for you to still be jealous.*

As Evergreen walked away, she heard Allaya say, "Boy, you are lucky I ran into you. If I had found out later you came to town and didn't tell me, you wouldn't have survived to New Year's."

CHAPTER 16

Lay-Lay turned her sparkling, dark eyes on Sawyer. "That girl still doesn't like me."

"Aw, come on, Lay-Lay. You're still going on about that after all this time?"

"Oh, don't get me wrong. I'm not taking it personally. It's your fault anyway."

"My fault? How?"

"How many times do I have to tell you? She only didn't like me because she liked you."

"You're crazy."

Lay-Lay smirked. "*I'm* crazy?"

She didn't have to elaborate. Sawyer understood her implication and sighed. "You were wrong, Lay-Lay. I have a lot of proof, as you know. And even if she had liked me back then, why would she still not like you?"

Lay-Lay raised her eyebrows significantly.

Sawyer felt his heart swell with hope, and he quickly tethered it before it flew away.

Lay-Lay smiled. "Look at that blush! You still like her. Don't you?" she teased.

Sawyer hushed her. "Yeah, I do. Okay?" he whispered. "Could you not broadcast it?"

She shook her head. "See? That has always been your problem. You were too quiet about your feelings. Maybe if you had been more honest, this whole thing could have been cleared up ages ago."

"Yeah, yeah."

Lay-Lay leaned forward, dropping her voice. "Do you want me to tell her for you? This whole thing could be over in ten seconds. Girl, Sawyer loves you. He's always loved you. I don't know where you got this idea he was into me. We have always just been friends. He's just shy. Take his coward ass home and give him some."

Sawyer's eyes scanned the room. "Lay-Lay," he admonished.

Lay-Lay sighed. "I know. Don't worry. I won't say anything. But I think you should. You two would be so cute together, raising your little Pagan babies."

"Oh my gods…"

"Who's that?" Lay-Lay asked, pointing behind Sawyer.

He looked over his shoulder at a man talking to Eeva. He looked vaguely familiar with his dark hair and olive skin, but Sawyer couldn't quite place him. His stomach clenched as Eeva smiled widely at the man, a pink blush dusting her cheeks. Eeva pointed toward their table.

"Well, we're about to find out. He's coming this way," Lay-Lay said.

"Hey, Collins. It's been a while. Good to see you," the man

said, holding out his hand to Sawyer.

"Yeah, it has. Nice to see you again," Sawyer said, trying and failing to place the man as he shook his hand. Sawyer glanced at Eeva. "I didn't know you two knew each other." *I definitely would have remembered a guy like him around Eeva,* he thought.

"Oh, Niko drove me home from the train station the other day. Apparently, his uncle owns this restaurant."

*Niko...Niko...*Sawyer searched his mind to place the name. *Oh, that guy from my summer photography class. The one all the girls were silly over.*

"Cool. I always loved this place," Sawyer said.

"Are you here for lunch, Niko?" Eeva asked. "You could join us if you want."

Sawyer's eyes snapped to Eeva's face then to Niko's.

"No, I'm just here to drop something off to my aunt."

"Oh," Eeva mumbled.

"But I could get a smoothie and sit with you guys for a bit," Niko added with a smooth smile.

Eeva perked up. "Great. This is Allaya. She was Sawyer's best friend in high school."

Lay-Lay and Niko greeted each other politely as Niko took the chair beside Eeva.

They were just starting to exchange basic information about what everyone did for a living when the waitress returned with their food.

"Oh, looks like they forgot my tzatziki sauce," Eeva said, putting her gyro down.

"You want me to call the waitress back?" Sawyer asked.

"No, it's fine. I can just go to the counter and ask for some."

She made her way toward the counter. Sawyer and Niko

watched her go. Halfway there, she bumped into an empty table. She paused, hissing as she rubbed her hip, then continued on.

Niko chuckled to himself. "She's a bit clumsy. Isn't she?"

"She's not clumsy. She's blind," Sawyer corrected coolly.

Niko blinked at him. "What?"

"Eeva is legally blind, and she has a habit of walking around without her cane."

Niko scrunched up his face, his attractive features twisted in disgust.

Sawyer's stomach dropped at the sight, and anger boiled in his chest. Lay-Lay stiffened beside him.

"Do you have a problem with that?" Sawyer challenged the man, his voice low and even.

Niko didn't seem to notice the rage bubbling just below the surface of Sawyer's tone. "No, I don't have a problem with someone being blind. I would just prefer to know that before I waste my interest on a girl."

"Everyone has something to deal with," Sawyer said, trying to keep his voice steady. "It's clear you struggle with an overinflated ego. You think you're so perfect that you can call her flawed? She was born that way. She had no choice in the matter. You weren't born a narcissistic prick, so what's your excuse? Eeva is beautiful inside and out. I'm glad you showed your true colors early on. You don't deserve her."

Niko slowly rose from his seat, hovering over Sawyer and tensing for a fight.

Sawyer stood up to meet him, barely aware that Lay-Lay had risen too as he looked down at the infuriated man. "Leave now. Before she gets back."

"This is my family's restaurant," Niko growled.

"And do you think your family would be pleased to know that this is how you treat disabled customers?"

Niko glared up at Sawyer, fury flashing in his dark eyes. Then, he turned on his heel and stormed away.

Sawyer took a deep breath and sat back down as Lay-Lay glared after Niko.

Drinking some Violet Rave, he glanced over at Lay-Lay, who had retaken her seat. She was staring at him seriously.

"What?" he asked, putting his cup down.

She grinned slowly. "My baby boy grew up. Look at you, all hot and manly. Why don't you show Eeva this side of you?"

Sawyer turned back to his meal without comment.

When Eeva returned to the table, she stopped short. "Where's Niko?"

"He had somewhere else to be," Sawyer answered.

"Oh. Damn. I wanted to hire him to take me home."

"Why would you need him to do that?"

"Well, I mean, you and Allaya haven't seen each other in a long time. I figured you would want more time to catch up."

Sawyer frowned. "Don't call him for a ride anymore. If you need someone to drive you somewhere, I'll take you."

Eeva's eyes widened, and she blinked a few times. "Um... Okay. Did something happen?"

"No," Sawyer said. *Maybe she knows there are men like him out there. But it would still be shocking and painful to be confronted head-on with something like this aimed directly at you. I don't think I could handle the hurt in her eyes.*

"Just let it go, girl. Let it go," Lay-Lay suggested.

CHAPTER 17

Evergreen looked over at Sawyer from the corner of her eye as he drove them home.

"I'm sorry you didn't get to spend more time with Allaya," she murmured.

"It's fine. She was only on her lunch break anyway," he said, his voice unconcerned.

"Do you…talk to her a lot?"

Sawyer turned his face toward her, just for a moment taking his eyes from the road. She jumped internally as his gaze unerringly found hers, if only for that second.

"I told you I didn't talk much with the people from school. We sometimes chat online every now and then. You know, just catch up or whatever."

Evergreen nodded slowly, her brain telling her to let it go. She didn't listen. "I'm just surprised. You two were so close."

"Yeah, we were. But then we went to separate colleges. It's

not like we aren't still friends. But things change when you don't see each other every day."

Yeah. Things change. Do you still feel the same way about her? Evergreen wondered. But she didn't give voice to her question.

"Still," he continued, "I think I can always count Allaya as one of my friends, no matter how long we don't talk or see each other. I guess at this point she's more like family. I mean, we've always called each other's moms 'mom.' And she only has sisters. Her family always wanted a boy. So I guess they just sort of adopted me in a way."

Evergreen stared hard at him, hoping she didn't look surly as she squinted to try and make out his features against the bright light outside the car. His face was restful, neither wrinkled with concern or joy. He appeared to just have stated the facts as he saw them.

Evergreen took a slow, quiet breath and turned her gaze to the snow-covered trees that lined the road. *He thinks of her as a sister? Could I have been wrong about them? But he was always smiling when he was around her, always laughing. He never smiled like that around me,* she thought. *Well, that just means that whatever joy she gave him as a friend and sibling, I didn't give him. Him not liking her in that way has no bearing on how he felt about me.*

"What are you thinking so hard about?" he asked.

"Nothing," she mumbled, wondering how he knew. "I'm just recalling some memories."

There was a thick silence before he said, "You know…Lay-Lay thinks you don't like her, that you never liked her."

Evergreen's heart squeezed. "Oh? Why is that?" she asked, trying to make her tone sound only curious.

Sawyer hesitated. "She said she thinks you don't like her because you think I like her…in a romantic way."

The sounds of the heater and the engine seemed more muffled as if Evergreen's ears were plugged. She held her breath as she became too aware of the blood pumping from her heart to her brain, the artery pulsing in her neck.

"But you just said you thought of her as family," she pointed out, her voice sounding weak and unconvincing to her own ears.

"Right," he agreed, equally quiet.

"And I have no reason to dislike Allaya. She has always been nice to me."

"I told her it wasn't true." He paused. "She's just paranoid," he added softly.

"But…" Evergreen hesitated. "I wouldn't have been surprised if you, or anyone for that matter, did like her that way. She's smart, pretty, and talented."

"She is all those things," he agreed. "But you can't control what your heart wants."

Evergreen dropped her gaze to her hands in her lap. "Yeah," she mumbled.

They rode the rest of the way back in silence, both lost in their own thoughts. The atmosphere in the car was thick and uncomfortable, and Evergreen was relieved when she stepped outside into the fresh, cold air.

"Aren't you coming in?" Sawyer asked when Evergreen made no move to head inside.

"I'm just going to go for a short walk," she said. "Will you take these in to my mom for me, please?"

Sawyer took the bag with the shampoo bottles from her with a nod and went inside.

Once he had closed the door, Evergreen took a deep breath. Then, she walked around the house to the back patio, the movement of walking calming her rattled mind. Without hesitating, she took the path into the woods, her boots crunching the pebbles on the frozen dirt.

"No. No, no, no," she murmured to herself. "Don't you dare, Evergreen."

She stopped, squinting up at the grey sky between the snow-laden branches of the trees all around her. She sighed; her chest warmed as Sawyer's words repeated in her mind. *You can't control what your heart wants.* She started walking again, faster, as if to outrun the phrase.

"He was just making a statement of fact," she told herself. "But…it had sounded so…heavy, so…suggestive. No, that's just what I *wanted* to hear. Wait…no it isn't. Why would I want to hear that?"

She followed the path up a steep hill to the small clearing where most of the coven's outdoor rituals took place, where they would have a bonfire, pitch tents, where her dedication had been. She plowed right through the clearing and descended the other side of the plateau.

"It doesn't matter," she insisted, her throat ragged as she took labored breaths of cold air. "It doesn't matter what he meant. Even if he came out tomorrow and told me he used to have a crush on me, that wouldn't change anything now. Right. It wouldn't change anything because a crush in the past means nothing in present day. And…I'm over him."

Her declaration sounded loud and final. Even insulated by

the surrounding woods, it seemed to echo as if she'd shouted it into an empty canyon. She stopped again, startled by the sudden feeling of intense loneliness. Looking around, she saw the edge of her family's property line. The small isolation cabin used for meditation and reflection marked the end of the retreat center.

She sighed again, and her stomach churned. She didn't follow her mind's train of thought. "I better get back," she mumbled. Then, she turned around and walked slowly home.

CHAPTER 18

Like the evening before, Sawyer sat at the coffee table beside Sol, sewing in the ends of the knitting projects his mom, Ria, and Eeva finished. Wes sat on the floor, decorating the baskets that would go to the shelter when they were all finished.

Sawyer peeked up at Eeva as she cast off the last row of the washcloth she was knitting. His heart panged as he recalled their earlier conversation.

What was I hoping for? he thought. *Why would I bring up her not liking Lay-Lay? The way her face flushed, she knew what I was suggesting. I knew she didn't like me. But when she asked about Lay-Lay, I just got the feeling that maybe...*

Evergreen looked up as she cut the tail off her project. She glanced at him and stilled as she realized he'd been watching her.

"This one is finished," she said, leaning forward to hand it to him.

He reached out, his fingers brushing hers as he took it from her. Her cheeks pinked ever so slightly, and warmth spread through him, heat pooling in his gut.

His manhood stiffened. Her hand had been soft and warm and real, not the hand of a long-ago crush. But the hand of present Eeva. The woman she had become, not the girl she had been.

She had changed. He had seen it, even in the two days they had spent together. She was much more contemplative, less likely to forge forward without thought. But her heart, it was the same. The way she interacted with her parents, her cousin, his mom, especially how she was with Sol. How she worried about failing to find a job, her laugh. Yes, she was different, but not so much that his heart wouldn't recognize her.

Let's not think about the past anymore, Sawyer told himself. *I've long known how I felt about her in the past. I want to know the new Eeva. And it's the future I should be concerned about. The past is already done. No, it doesn't matter how she felt about me back then. It's how she feels now that matters.*

"Uncle Wes," Sol said, pulling Sawyer from his contemplations.

"Yes, Sparkler," Wes answered, pausing in his decorating.

"Will you tell us a story? My mom always says you were the best at storytelling."

Wes smiled. "Your mom was always the best listener."

"Hey, I listened," Eeva countered.

"You did when you could sit still long enough," Cassandra said.

"Point taken," Eeva conceded.

"Hmm. Let's see. What sort of story should I tell?" He sat on the floor, facing those assembled.

"There once was a wise and powerful sun god, and he was married to an equally wise and powerful earth goddess," Wes started.

"Did the god and goddess have names?" Sol asked.

Wes nodded. "They have had many names, too many to list. The goddess and god were very happy together, and their joy brought new life to the earth. In the spring, the god impregnated the goddess with his seed. As the seed grew, so did all the plants on earth, warmed by the love they shared. The seeds grew so big that they began to sprout and bear fruit. And the people and animals were happy because they had a lot to eat."

"But what about now?" Sol asked. "All the plants are sleeping."

"That's right," Wes said. "Because death is the inevitable part of life. The god died on Samhain, and the goddess was very sad. The plants slowly died with him, and the sun didn't warm the earth the way it used to."

Sol frowned, tears filling his eyes.

"But, even though he died, he left something behind: the seed he left with the goddess. Because when something dies, that death only fuels new life for those it leaves behind."

"What happened to the seed?" Sol asked.

"On Yule, the winter solstice, the seed was reborn as a new sun god. The days got longer, and the sun got warmer. And eventually, the goddess was renewed as well. That's why, every year, the people celebrate the changing of the seasons. And at Yule, we celebrate the birth of the new sun god and the return of the light."

"I hope he isn't late," Sol said. "Mom said sometimes babies come late. She said I was three whole days late."

Sawyer stifled a laugh. "Don't worry, my friend," he told the boy. "He won't be late."

Sol pursed his lips and squinted his eyes. "Are you sure?"

Sawyer nodded seriously. "Positive. The god always returns just when he says he will."

"Okay," Sol agreed, apparently reassured.

Shortly after Wes had finished his story, Cassandra took Sol up to bed. It wasn't long before everyone else called it a night as well, leaving Eeva and Sawyer alone in the common room.

"You're up late," Sawyer pointed out. "Aren't you tired? You were up before everyone else this morning too."

Eeva yawned. "Yeah, I just know I won't be able to get to sleep."

"Something on your mind?"

Eeva frowned and sighed, wrapping up her knitting and putting it aside. "It's more like trying to keep something off my mind. If that makes any sense."

"Do you want to talk about it? Maybe it will help."

She glanced at him. He put on a reassuring expression, though he wasn't sure how much of his face she could see from that distance.

"You ever have something you just don't want to face? I mean, you know when you get a tarot reading where every card just tells you exactly what you already know, but you don't want to accept it? If you hadn't pulled the cards, could you have just gone on pretending, ignoring the truth?"

Sawyer thought about it for a moment. "I always find facing the truth is the best option. If I ignore it, it's not like it will go away. The longer I wait to face it, the harder it's going to be to deal with because it's just growing there in the dark."

Eeva sighed again. "I had a feeling you'd say something like that… But what if you aren't ready to face it?"

"Hard to say. I mean, I'd never suggest you overextend yourself or force yourself to deal with something you aren't ready for. But on the other hand, sometimes we don't have much of a choice. Sometimes things just happen, and we have to deal with them whether we're ready or not."

Eeva nodded slowly.

"So, which do you think it is? Do you think you have the luxury of ignoring it for the time being?" Sawyer asked.

"I'm not sure," she said. "But it will hold until tomorrow at least. I think I'm going to go up and try to sleep."

Sawyer nodded. "Sleep well," he said.

"Thanks. You too."

But just as she stood up to leave, Sawyer called out to her. "Hey, Eeva, since the suet is finished, do you want to go out and feed the animals with me tomorrow? I'm hoping to get some good pictures."

Eeva paused, and Sawyer held his breath.

"Sure," she said finally.

Warmth spread through Sawyer as he grinned. He was grateful that she left without turning back to see the stupid look on his face.

CHAPTER 19

After breakfast the next morning, Evergreen and Sawyer started putting on their coats and hats to go outside.

"Where are you two off to?" Ria asked, as everyone watched them from the living room.

"We're going to put out the suet for the birds," Evergreen answered her mother. "And Sawyer wants to see if he can get some wildlife photos."

"In that case, would you like some chestnuts for the squirrels, too?" Wes asked.

"That would be great," Sawyer answered.

"Since you're going out, would you mind gathering some things for the door wreath?" Ria asked.

"No problem," Evergreen said.

"Great. I'll go get the basket," Ria responded.

"I want to come too," Sol said, standing from his place at the coffee table.

"I thought you wanted to work on your art for the baskets, Sol," his mother pointed out before Evergreen could agree.

Sol was silent for a moment. Evergreen could practically hear him weighing his thoughts, though she couldn't see his expression from across the room.

"You're right, Mama. I'm sorry, Eeva. But I can't go with you this time. I have too much work to do," Sol apologized sincerely.

Evergreen smiled, managing to hold back her laugh at his serious tone. "That's all right, Sparkler. I understand. I'll see you later. Okay?"

"Okay," he agreed.

As her mother handed her the basket and chestnuts, Evergreen asked, "Have you seen Muir?"

"He's over there by the fire sleeping with Larkspur," she told her.

"Oh, good. If he wakes up and starts crying, it's because he wants attention. I have some toys up in my room for him."

"I think I know how to take care of my grandcat, Evergreen," Ria said flatly.

"I know. I just don't want him to wake up and be looking for me."

"He'll be fine," she assured.

"Make sure he doesn't eat any of Larkspur's food. He's on a special diet, and I don't want him to get sick."

"If you don't leave this house right now, I'm going to kick you out," her mother warned.

"Fine. We're going."

"Here, take this, too," Wes said, coming out from the kitchen and holding an insulated lunch box out to Sawyer. "There are sandwiches and a Thermos of cocoa."

"Dad, we aren't going to be gone that long. We aren't even leaving the property."

"Yeah, well, time can get away from you," he said with a shrug.

Sawyer thanked Wes and smiled.

"I don't need to tell you to watch where you're going," Ria warned Evergreen. "I see you don't have your cane with you. Pay attention to where you're walking. Take it slow. Sawyer, you'll watch out for her, won't you?"

"Mom, seriously, I was just out there by myself yesterday. I think I know the woods I grew up in by now."

"Things grow and change, Miss Smarty Pants," Ria snarked.

"All right, we're out of here," Evergreen declared.

The rest called their goodbyes.

As he closed the door behind them, Sawyer turned to Evergreen with a smile. And they shared a small chuckle.

"You ready?" he asked, his camera bag on one shoulder and the lunch bag on the other.

Evergreen nodded, lifting the basket she'd put the suet and chestnuts into.

"What's easier for you?" Sawyer asked. "Is it easier for you to go first or me?"

"You can go first," Evergreen said, reluctantly heeding her mother's warning. "Just warn me if there are any unexpected holes or tree roots."

He agreed and started on toward the path she had taken the day before.

Once they were in the woods and the house was out of sight,

it grew very quiet. The birds still chirped sporadically in the distance, and there was still the odd skittering sound of creatures just beyond sight. But Sawyer's presence was heavy, like a weighted blanket on her chest. The analogous crunching of their footfalls wasn't enough to relieve the pressure.

Evergreen looked up from scrutinizing the path and watched Sawyer as he marched on before her. She couldn't see his golden hair under his beanie, and his neck was covered by a striped scarf, one his mother no doubt crocheted for him. His shoulders were wide under his winter coat, much wider than she remembered. *He really filled out over the last few years,* Evergreen thought.

Her eyes traveled down to the back of his jeans, and the thought surfaced in her mind before she could stop it. *His ass is nice, too.* Her face flushed, and her ears radiated heat under her hat. She focused her gaze on the path in front of her, concentrating on every step. *Oh my gods, no. That's not okay.*

"Are you all right?" Sawyer asked, his head turned over his shoulder at her. "Do you need to take a break?"

"No, why?" she murmured.

"Because your breathing sounds more labored than before, and your face is all red. Do I need to slow down? Am I walking too fast?"

"I'm fine," she assured. "I just have too many layers on." She unwrapped the scarf from her neck and shoved it into her coat pocket.

"Okay," he said, his tone free of suspicion.

"So, are there any particular birds you're hoping to get pictures of?" Evergreen asked, filling the silence so her mind wouldn't go on its own.

"Not really," he answered noncommittally. After a short pause, he added, "I'm sorry, Eeva."

He stopped walking, and she halted so as not to run into him. He turned to face her.

"I feel like I invited you out here under false pretenses." He raised his eyes from the ground to meet hers. "I mean…I still want to get some pictures, but I was just using the tradition of feeding the animals as a way to spend more time with you."

Evergreen's heart thumped hard in her ears, and her breath came out in long puffs of frosted air. *Spend more time with me,* she thought. *Why would you want to do that?* She wanted to ask him. She wanted the answer. *What would he say? He wanted to catch up, like he mentioned before? He has a favor to ask of me? He missed me?* The potential answers varied vastly.

Evergreen gave him her best polite smile. "That's okay," she said, accepting his apology. "It's nice to get outside and enjoy the season. I've been cooped up far too much with schoolwork and job hunting lately. And I always enjoyed feeding the animals."

Sawyer watched her. She couldn't make out his expression, but she doubted it gave much away.

Her mind raged at her. *You fucking coward.*

CHAPTER 20

Sawyer stared at Eeva's professional smile. There was no warmth in it. *Did she just...?* His mind analyzed her reaction. *But she isn't angry. She isn't upset. Distant, formal, yes, but that could be caution. Eeva never had a problem with confrontation or standing up and raising her voice to fight for what is right when she thought it could help others. But when it came to something that was only for herself, she was always more reluctant, bashful almost. Did I embarrass her by saying that? But I want her to know how I feel. Fine. If she needs me to ease in, to take it slow, I can do that. But I'm not going to mince words this time. Until she indicates she isn't interested, I'm going to be open and honest about how I'm feeling toward her.*

"Thanks," Sawyer said finally. "I wanted to be honest."

Eeva nodded. "Should we keep going then? We've still got a bit before we reach the clearing."

"Yeah," Sawyer agreed and turned back around to lead the way.

As they walked, Sawyer was acutely aware of Eeva behind him. He focused on the sound of her footsteps, on the quiet hush of her even breathing. The weight of her presence was as if she was leaning against his back, embracing him from behind. And every so often, a tingle would run up his spine as if he felt the brush of a kiss on the back of his neck, and he knew her eyes were on him.

Eventually, they came to the clearing and approached the first suet cage hanging from a branch. Sawyer reached up and took the cage off the chain. Then, he opened it, and Eeva popped suet cubes into it. There were two other cages, and they repeated the action at each.

"Where do you think we should put the chestnuts? On the altar?" Eeva asked.

"Yeah, I think that works fine."

They moved to the big stone that the coven had often used as an altar during outdoor rituals. Sawyer used his gloved hands to brush the snow from the surface. Eeva took the bag of raw chestnuts from the basket and piled its contents onto the cleared stone.

"Do you want to gather the wreath stuff now? If we leave the clearing, there might be some animals to take pictures of by the time we come back this way," Eeva asked.

"That's a good idea," Sawyer agreed.

He led the way down the hill, warning Eeva that the trail sloped down and to watch out for tree roots. The tone of her acknowledgement led him to believe that she was aware of the obstacles he pointed out. But she had asked him to warn her, so he did.

"What about that fir over there?" Sawyer said, pointing a little off the path.

Evergreen raised an eyebrow at him. "Really?" she asked. "You think you're just going to point, and I'm magically going to be able to see that far?"

Sawyer chuckled. "Sorry. That was silly."

"Don't worry about it. Sometimes I even forget I'm blind." She laughed. "But yeah, fir sounds good. Lead the way."

Sawyer went on ahead, warning Eeva about every fallen stick and holding branches out of the way so she wouldn't hit her face.

Once they'd reached the tree, they stopped, appreciating it for a moment.

"I'll look for pinecones," Eeva said, dropping down to search the ground.

"All right. I'll take a cutting then." Sawyer pulled out his pocketknife and reached toward the tree. "Oh great and sturdy evergreen," he murmured. "You who represent hope and renewable life. You promise the return of spring. Please lend us some of your life to get us through the darkness of winter." He paused for a moment, just existing in the tree's presence. It was calm, and a low frequency tingle hummed in Sawyer's veins. "Thank you for your sacrifice," Sawyer told the tree. "It will not go unappreciated."

Then he cut a few ends to accent the Yule wreath they were making.

Eeva held out the basket for him, and he could see she had a couple pinecones in it already.

"So, what else do you think? Cedar would be nice. It would be easy to work with, too," she said.

Sawyer nodded. "I'll look for one. Let's go back to the path."

They carefully made their way back and continued walking down the trail.

"There's one," Sawyer declared. "And right near the path, too."

"Awesome. Let's get some."

The pair approached the tree, and Sawyer repeated the process of communing with the plant. But as he reached up and cut one of the thin branches, some of the snow from the nearby branches shook off and fell onto Eeva's head.

"Oh! That's cold," Eeva complained, wiggling to get the snow off her.

Sawyer laughed at the sight. "Well, why did you stand under where I was cutting then? You deserve it," he teased.

"I deserve it, eh?" Eeva asked, grinning. She placed the basket on the ground and gathered a handful of snow. "Then, I guess you deserve this!" She threw the snow into his face.

"Oh, it's on now," he said, shaking his head, trying to get the snow out from the inside of his scarf.

Eeva laughed and threw another snowball.

The battle raged on. They each got some good shots in. Eeva had surprisingly good aim for someone who couldn't see well. But Sawyer made sure to make some noise to indicate his position. It wouldn't be fair otherwise.

They ran up and down the path, laughter and squeals dampened by the surrounding trees. Finally, they lay on their backs beside each other on the ground, breathless and covered in snow.

"Truce?" Sawyer asked, turning his head toward her.

She turned her head and met his eyes. She sat up, gathered a giant pile of snow between her hands, and dumped it right onto his face.

"Yeah," she giggled. "Truce." She collapsed back down beside him.

He sat up and tried to shake the snow from him but gave up and lay back down. "That was uncalled for," he complained.

Eeva rolled over on her side to face him more completely, propping her elbow on the ground and resting her head in her hand. "Well, you started the whole thing, so I had to finish it."

"I didn't start it. The tree started…" his words trailed off as Eeva reached out and brushed snow from his hat.

His breath caught. She didn't smile at him. Her face was smooth, and her lips slightly parted. Her deep blue eyes were trained on him, serious and intense as she looked down at him.

He'd seen that look before but never from her. He had only dreamed, only fantasized, about ever seeing that heated look from Eeva.

His heart thumped hard in his chest, pumping heat through his veins. His cock throbbed to life, raised by the desire in her eyes.

"Eeva," he whispered, tensing to sit up, ready to meet her, ready to give her what her expression said she wanted.

She blinked, and her eyebrows crinkled. The sound of her name seemed to shake her out of the moment. She pulled her hand back, frowning.

Sawyer's own desire waned at the sight of her change in demeanor. *She's not ready,* he told himself. *But I saw it. I know it's there. I can wait.*

CHAPTER 21

After they had gone back to the basket and finished collecting cedar boughs, Evergreen suggested they warm up and have lunch in the isolation cabin, which wasn't too far away from where they were.

Sawyer agreed, and Evergreen led the way since he didn't remember where it was.

Upon reaching the cabin, Eeva took the spare key from its hiding place and unlocked the door.

The cabin was small and chilled. It consisted of a single room plus a bathroom. In the main room, there was a fireplace, a coffee table, and a chest with blankets in it. At the far end, there was a kitchenette with a single burner on the counter and a sink. The cupboard above the sink had some snacks and a few dishes. It was a place meant for quiet reflection and meditation, a place where someone could be alone and learn to be comfortable with that.

Sawyer stood in the doorway, taking the space in. Evergreen looked over her shoulder at him.

"Something wrong?" she asked.

"No," he answered, stepping in and closing the door behind him. "I just haven't been here in a long time. I think I was only ever here once at that."

Evergreen glanced around the space. "Doesn't seem to have changed much," she said with a shrug. "Anyway, we won't be here long, so I won't make a fire. But the cocoa should warm us up soon enough."

She unzipped her coat and removed her wet hat and gloves. Sawyer did the same. As Sawyer unpacked the lunch box onto the short table, Evergreen went to the cupboard for an extra mug for the cocoa.

"Look at that," Sawyer laughed. "Your dad even put a can of whipped cream and a baggie of chocolate chips in here."

"He knows me well." Evergreen smiled and sat at the opposite side of the table from Sawyer.

As they settled into their meal, Evergreen glanced up at Sawyer only for a second before looking back at the whipped cream in her cup.

Why did I do that? she wondered. *That was just stupid. I should have had better control. But...*

She pictured Sawyer's face again, looking up at her from the ground, snow clumped to his hat and scarf.

I've never seen his face so close before. The closest I've ever gotten to seeing him in detail was photos. And it's different in person. He was...real. Warm and real, and I couldn't help but wonder what it would be like to kiss him.

Evergreen paused in her chewing, shaking her head.

It's a good thing he said my name and jolted me out of it. I might have done something I shouldn't have.

His voice echoed in her mind. *"Eeva..."* There was no mistaking the heat in that word. It had been thick and heavy and was all too like the whispers she'd heard countless times in her dreams.

Yes, in the feverish dreams of a lovesick teenager. Not the dreams of a grown woman who is too smart to go down that road again. Nope, there's no place for Sawyer Collins in my life anymore. I mean...he clearly wanted to kiss me. A moment longer and it would have happened. But then what? He has a whole life I'm not a part of. He has a job, which is gods know where. For all I know he has a girlfriend, too. No, we're so far past that point. I can't allow someone who had so much control over my heart in again. It's better to keep my distance. I need to have control of the situation.

Evergreen glanced at him again, glad he wasn't looking at her. *Okay, it's clear I'm still attracted to him. But so what? That's not a problem. I was attracted to him before, and I managed just fine.*

A small voice in her head countered her point. *But you were only fighting your own desire last time, not his.*

Evergreen took a deep drink from her mug, the hot liquid burning her throat on the way down.

It's not a problem, she assured herself. *It was only a fleeting thing on his part and a momentary lapse on mine. I mean, I'm not unattractive. Why wouldn't a man want to kiss me? That doesn't really mean anything. No, no, next time I won't let it get that far. Next time... Wait...no, there won't be a next time. After Yule, it won't be likely that I'll see him again, not unless the coven gets together for another sabbat. And that isn't likely anytime soon. No, we probably won't see each other for a long time after this.*

Evergreen's heart squeezed, and she couldn't ignore it. *See? This is a problem. Already, after just a few days, I'm upset about not seeing him again. I definitely need to keep my distance. I won't go through that heartbreak again.*

Evergreen and Sawyer ate their lunch in silence, the isolation cabin hollow with only the sounds of quiet chewing and the occasional slurp of cocoa drinking. After they were finished, Evergreen washed the extra mug and put it away.

"We should head back soon," Evergreen murmured.

Sawyer nodded. "It should have been enough time that the birds and squirrels have found our offerings."

"Right. Well then, let's see if you can get the pictures you want." Evergreen shut and locked the door of the isolation cabin and put the key back in its place.

The pair walked in silence through the woods. Their pace was slow, and they told themselves that it was not to scare any animals away. But it took them a lot longer to reach the clearing than it should have.

They crouched down, peeking over the hill to see if they had any visitors.

"Anything?" Evergreen whispered, unable to see that far. She squinted, trying to make out movement.

"There's a squirrel," Sawyer murmured back as he took the lens cap from his camera lens.

After a few snaps of the shutter, he looked down at the screen then turned the camera to her. She squinted at the screen, holding it close to her face. There was a grey squirrel with a big fluffy tail. He held a chestnut between his little paws.

"Aww, look at him. He's so cute," she said, grinning at the picture. "Are there any birds?"

Sawyer looked over the hill again and shook his head.

"Do you want to wait and see what we can get?" she asked.

"Do you mind? You're not too cold, are you?"

"I'm fine for a while," she assured.

After over an hour, their only reward was a few shots of a finch and a couple of blurry sparrows.

Sawyer glanced over at her as the sparrows flew away. "Let's call it a day, huh?"

"Are you sure?" she asked.

He nodded. "Yeah, it's getting cold out here. And besides, if your nose gets any redder, it might fall off."

Evergreen held her glove to her nose, and Sawyer chuckled. The sound was rich and warm. *Eeva...* he whispered in her mind, desire coloring his voice with heat.

"Yeah, let's head in," she agreed.

CHAPTER 22

*A*fter dinner had been cleared from the table and Cassandra and Tara were doing the dishes, Sawyer and Eeva brought the supplies they'd gathered to the dining room. Wes set out some crafting paper.

"You found some really good stuff this time," Ria complimented, carefully removing the boughs and pinecones from the basket and setting them on the paper.

Wes nodded. "I'll go get the wreath ring and the twine."

With well-practiced hands, Ria and Wes assembled the bits of greenery into a beautiful Yule wreath in less than an hour. As they worked, Sawyer and Eeva used the other side of the table to help Sol make his suncatcher.

When the wreath was complete, Sawyer took it to the front porch and hung it on the prepared hook. He walked down the front steps and turned around to better appreciate it from a distance. He nodded with a satisfied smile.

Everyone else was just settling down to the evening knitting when he returned. He took up residence beside Sol in his customary place.

"Eeva," Ria said. "I'm going to need you to move your things from the attic down to the meditation room first thing in the morning. Everyone will be arriving tomorrow, and I have to make sure the room is clean."

"What? Why?"

"Evergreen Pendre, you know we only have so much space. I warned you that you might have to sleep on the floor. And Devan and Piper need the single rooms. You know Devan has a CPAP machine, and Piper's snoring could wake the dead."

"But..." Eeva's protests trailed off.

Sawyer studiously kept his eyes on his work and tried to maintain a smooth expression. But he strained his ears to hear over the beating of his heart.

"What are you worried about?" Wes asked. "You, Cassandra, and Sawyer used to share a tent all the time."

"Maybe she's worried one of us will walk in on them," Cassandra suggested.

Sawyer glanced at Eeva out of the corner of his eye. Her cheeks were pink as she squinted at her cousin.

"Oh, don't worry about that, honey," Ria said. "Just lock the door."

"Mom!" Eeva moaned, her face completely flushed.

"What?" Ria asked. "There's nothing wrong with it. You're both adults. As long as it's consensual, there's no problem."

"Stop...talking..." Eeva mumbled, covering her face with her hands.

"Eeva, we didn't teach you to be ashamed of these types of

discussions," Wes said. "Your mother is right. Sex is a natural act. There's no reason to behave like this."

"Okay, it's a natural act. That doesn't mean I want to talk about it with my parents in front of everybody. And anyways, it's not right for you to suggest something like that would happen between Sawyer and I without taking our feelings into consideration."

Silence answered her.

"I'm sorry," Cassandra said finally. "I was just teasing, but I didn't mean for you to get this upset. We always used to joke about you and Sawyer getting together. I thought it would be okay."

Eeva sighed. "Things are…different now," she said.

How are they different? Sawyer wondered. *Why was it okay then but not now? Is it because now she's attracted to me? Now there is some semblance of a chance that it could happen?*

"In any case," Ria continued. "You still need to move your things to the meditation room."

"Fine," Eeva muttered.

The rest of the evening was fairly quiet, giving Sawyer's active thoughts no distraction.

As he lay on the floor in his sleeping bag, he stared at the clear night sky through the glass roof of the meditation room. The low whir of the space heater barely even registered.

"Things are different now," he murmured to himself, repeating Eeva's words from earlier that evening.

He had to agree with her. Before, things hadn't felt so real. He'd never been in a relationship before. He'd been a virgin. All of his ideas of what could happen with Eeva had been juvenile and, in some cases, downright inaccurate.

But now, they had both learned and experienced things. There wasn't the same shyness that came with stepping cautiously into the unknown.

The jokes about them being together from their teenage years felt far away, truly fantastical. And though he had wanted them to become reality, he knew now that he hadn't the courage to make it so back then.

Sawyer's dream that night was a complex mixture of memory and fantasy, the kind where his conscious mind somehow marked the deviations from the past but wasn't aware enough to change the course of the dream.

The spring night was warm, and the window to Sawyer's dorm room was open. A hard knock sounded on his door, and he called that it was unlocked.

His friend Felicity walked in at his beckon.

"I can't believe it," she said. "You really aren't going to go?"

He glanced up from his phone as he lounged on his bed. "I said I wasn't."

"Yeah, but I didn't believe you."

"I didn't go last year either."

"What is your deal with Beltaine anyway? You go to all the other rituals with no problem." Felicity climbed up on the bed, shooing his feet so she could sit down.

Sawyer didn't answer but glanced back at his phone. He stared at a picture of Eeva, a wreath of spring flowers in her hair. It had been posted a half hour ago.

Felicity crawled up beside him on the bed, peeking at his phone. She groaned. "Oh, come on, dude. Not this again."

"Leave me alone, Flick," he said, turning the phone away from her.

"It has been what? Like a year and a half since you even talked to her? When are you going to give up?"

He didn't respond. He didn't even know the answer himself.

"You know, there are a lot of women trying to get your attention if you would just get your head out of your ass long enough to see them."

Sawyer snorted. "Yeah, right."

"Dude, I'm serious. Shelby is practically begging for it."

Sawyer glanced over at his friend. There was no trace of joking on her face.

"I'm not really in a place where I can be with anyone. It wouldn't be right with my head all full of…Eeva."

"Ugh, you're so honorable. It's disgusting," Felicity moaned sarcastically.

"Well, excuse me for being a decent human being."

"You are not excused."

Sawyer laughed. Felicity always had a way of making him laugh.

"Maybe you just need to, I don't know, get her out of your system. You know?"

"Yeah? How am I going to do that?"

"You're way too fixated. Loosen up, branch out, get to know some other people. You might like Shelby if you gave her a chance."

"Yeah, and I might get intimate with her and call out someone else's name. How fucked up would that be?"

Felicity paused for a long time before she asked, "Is that what you need to do?"

"What?"

"Do you need to be with someone else and pretend it's her?"

"That's just wrong."

"It's not if the other person consents to it… I'd do it. I mean, don't get me wrong, dude, I don't want you to think I'm, like, into you or anything. But I'm your friend, and I don't like seeing you like this. We could do it on Beltaine and just go on with our lives tomorrow. I wouldn't want your first time to be all emotionally complicated or whatever anyway."

Sawyer's heart pounded, and his mouth went dry. He stared at Felicity, wondering if she was serious.

Then the memory shifted from reality. He wasn't in his dorm room; he was in the clearing at the retreat center. The Beltaine fire was built high; it would burn through the night.

Eeva was in Felicity's place. But it wasn't Eeva from his memories. It was the Eeva from the present. She did all the things Felicity had done. And it wasn't the purely physical release it had been; it was everything he'd wanted. He didn't have to pretend, and love shone in her eyes.

CHAPTER 23

The next morning, as Evergreen packed her things to move them downstairs, she wondered if Sawyer knew why she didn't want to share a room with him.

I have a hard enough time maintaining balance with him around when I have my own space to retreat to, she thought. *It's fine. I can do this. I'm in complete control over my actions.*

She pushed aside the thought that it was her emotions she had no control over.

She carried her things downstairs, hesitating at the door to the meditation room. She could hear her dad already puttering around in the kitchen. And Cassandra was curled up on the couch watching cartoons with Sol.

She knocked gently to be sure Sawyer wasn't in there. Her knock received no reply, so she opened the door.

On the floor, Sawyer still lay asleep in his sleeping bag. As Sol's laughter filtered in from the other room, Evergreen gently shut the door behind her.

She crept to one side and carefully placed her suitcase and Muir's litter box on the floor.

Just as she turned to leave, Sawyer groaned in his sleep. She halted and went back, looking down at him.

Is he sick? she wondered. *Is he having a nightmare?*

Evergreen knelt down beside him. Sawyer's face was moist with sweat, his hair stuck to his forehead. He squeezed his eyes shut. His breathing was heavy and uneven. She reached out her hand and placed the back gingerly on his cheek. He didn't seem to be running a fever. *A nightmare then?*

"Eeva..." he whispered, his voice breathless and moaning.

She pulled her hand back with a start, certain she had awoken him. But his eyes remained closed.

He called her name again, and a shiver ran up her spine. It sounded too much like how he'd said it the day before, too much like how he'd said it in her dreams the previous night.

Feelings from her dreams, feelings she'd thought she had successfully washed away with cool water, surfaced in her mind. Eeva didn't dream like other people. She didn't see images like they did in the movies in any case. She always thought that it was because she didn't see very well. But in her dreams, she didn't see at all. She didn't even really hear. She just felt and knew. She knew people by their presence rather than their faces or the sound of their voices.

It wasn't really strange for her when she started to dream about her first time. She often did when she was sexually flustered. What was strange was the love she'd felt for Tyler in the dream. Oh, she liked him okay enough, and she had certainly been attracted to him. But she hadn't loved him, which is why they broke up in the end.

The dream started out as usual, Tyler and her making out in the woods behind the humanities building. But just as Tyler had steadied her weight against the trunk of a particularly thick oak, the dream shifted. The lust she'd felt was overshadowed by the feeling that this is what she'd always wanted. And as Tyler had smiled down at her, and she met the outpouring of his love with hers, she realized it wasn't Tyler at all. It was Sawyer. And he whispered her name in a low moan, just as he was doing now.

As the feeling resurfaced, Evergreen reminded herself that it was just a dream. She had had many sexual dreams about her guy friends over the years. And once she was fully awake and in the light of day, the feelings in those dreams always faded out of existence.

Maybe it has been too long, she thought, trying to count how long it had been since she'd broken up with Dean. She hadn't even gotten that far with Marty. *Yeah, too long. This Yuletide reunion couldn't have happened at a worse time.*

She looked down at Sawyer again. His breathing had evened out, and he no longer seemed to be dreaming. As quietly as she could, she rose and left the room.

"Is Sawyer awake?" Ria asked as Evergreen entered the living room.

"No."

"Will you go wake him, please? It's time for breakfast."

"I'll do it!" Sol said, running off in that direction.

A few seconds later, Sol's voice sounded from the other room. "Sawyer, it's time to get up!"

There was a shout and a thud.

Shortly after, Sol emerged. "He's awake," he declared brightly, clearly proud of the job he'd done.

Sawyer entered after the boy. Even Evergreen could see his hair was mussed as his socked feet shuffled on the floor.

"Well, good morning, son," Tara said. "You look wrung out. Didn't you sleep well?"

Sawyer paused for a while. "It was fine," he murmured, his voice still thick with sleep.

His mother sounded unconvinced. "Uh-huh. Well, get some food in you so you can shower before people start arriving. You look like you just escaped from being held hostage."

At breakfast, Sawyer sat across from Evergreen as Sol insisted that it was his turn to sit beside her. Sawyer didn't tease the boy. Didn't say much of anything, in fact. And as they all tucked into their French toast, Evergreen glanced over at him.

He was eating, slow and deliberate.

She squinted, trying to make out his expression. *What's he thinking about?* she wondered.

Sawyer glanced up, meeting her eyes for just a moment. Evergreen froze, her body flushing as his heated gaze bespoke his thoughts. He looked back down, the exchange taking only a second.

What the hell was that? she wondered, dropping her eyes to her own food. But she wasn't stupid, she knew what it was. And even worse, she recognized her very real reaction to it. She shivered once as if his releasing her gaze had left her out in the cold.

Glancing back at him again, she bit her lip. *Sharing a room with him is going to be much harder than I thought.*

CHAPTER 24

Sawyer chided himself internally. *Why did you do that? Get a grip. You're having breakfast for gods' sakes.*

Sawyer glanced up at Eeva again, carefully controlling his expression. But she wasn't looking at him. She stared down at her French toast as if it took all her concentration to eat it.

A vivid image from his dream flashed into his mind, Eeva's face stiff with pleasure, her eyes boring into his as he thrust deep inside her.

His cock throbbed. He dropped his fork, and a loud clang sounded through the dining room when it hit his plate.

As everyone's attention turned toward him, he pushed back from the table. "I'm, uh, not that hungry. I think I'll just go take a shower and eat later. Thanks for breakfast though."

He didn't wait for their responses before making his escape. Using the movement to push all thoughts aside, he gathered his clothes and headed to the bathroom.

Sawyer stepped under the rainfall showerhead and let the

warmth of the water ease his tense muscles. His sigh echoed off the stone walls of the grotto-style shower. He'd kept the lighting in the bathroom low, only turning on the small, dim bulb in the shower itself.

As he began to relax, more images from his dream arose in his mind. He clenched his teeth together, stifling a groan. His balls ached as his cock strained to get larger than his skin allowed.

He sighed again, slowly, puffing his cheeks out as the hot water streamed down his face. Then he reached for the conditioner and squeezed a decent amount of the thick cream into his right palm.

Closing his eyes, he braced his left hand against the stone wall in front of him and hung his head. The water hit the back of his head, gathering in his hair before dripping into his eyes and down his neck.

He let the myriad of images flow and closed his hand around the shaft of his throbbing cock. He shuddered, the combination of the pressure from his hand and the warmth from the water sending a jolt of pleasure through him.

Eeva's hair smelled of lotus as he buried his face in its soft waves. Her breath was hot and uneven in his ear. He could feel the weight of her in his lap, and his hands glided easily over the smooth skin of her back.

"Sawyer," she whispered his name. "*Come for me,*" she begged.

As he tensed and shuddered and his released desire pumped out of him, he swallowed his moan of satisfaction.

He sighed then took a few deep breaths, pressing his fingertips into the rough wall of the shower.

He'd long lost count of how many times Eeva had featured

in his sexual fantasies. But this time felt different. The look she'd given him the day before, her flushed face at breakfast, never had his fevered daydreams been so close within reach.

With his sexual tension released, his mind dwelled on foggy recollections of why his heart had never let her go. The kind witch who could laugh with the carefree lightness of an untroubled soul, whose eyes flashed as she stood up to face her peers and elders when she felt an injustice had been done, who cried at others' pain be they human, animal, or plant. She had long enchanted him.

He knew any distance she set between herself and the world was only to protect her tender heart. She cared too deeply, felt too much. It was a very real problem for an empath. He had long watched her slowly build her walls, brick by mental brick. If he knocked on the door, would she let him in? He knew she was capable of protecting herself, but still… Couldn't he protect her, too? Was that so wrong?

After his shower, Sawyer dressed and finished getting ready for the day. As he entered the sitting room, he asked Ria if she needed any help preparing the lodge for everyone else to arrive.

She looked over from the mantle while she fussed over the ivy not being evenly distributed. "No, no. You're fine, hon. You're a guest too after all. And I really don't have much left to do. We already changed the sheets in the attic. And Cassandra is up there vacuuming now."

"Well, would you like anything to drink? I'm heading to the kitchen," he offered.

"Actually, I'll have a cup of tea if you're putting the kettle on. Thank you, Sawyer. You've always been so thoughtful."

As Sawyer made his way to the kitchen, the doorbell

chimed. The sound of feet thumped rhythmically on the stairs before Eeva and Sol appeared.

"I got it," Eeva called as she raced the boy to the door.

"Evergreen, Sol, don't run on the stairs," Ria chided. "What if one of you fell?"

Curious to see who had arrived, Sawyer trailed after them.

"Uh, Mom…?" Eeva called, hesitating as she stood beside Sol in the doorway.

Sawyer came up behind them and looked over Eeva's shoulder. A smiling young man, probably in his late 20s early 30s, stood on the porch. He wore a well-kept suit with a tie and a winter overcoat. In his hand, he held a black leather book and a stack of glossy papers.

"What?" Ria shouted from the other room.

"Um, there's a Jehovah's Witness out here," Eeva called back.

Seconds later, Ria arrived at the threshold.

"I couldn't help but notice the wreath on your door," the man said. "Do you have a moment? I'd like to talk to you about Christmas."

Ria tilted her head. "Are you new to this area?" she asked the man.

"Yes." He smiled. "My wife and I just moved to Birchland with our baby boy."

"Oh, well, welcome to the neighborhood. I'm Ria Pendre. My husband and I own this retreat center. Would you like to come in for a cup of tea? We were just about to put the kettle on. You're a ways from town way out here, and it's pretty chilly out."

"I'd love to, ma'am," the man said. "Thank you very much. I'm Caleb."

"Well, come on in, Caleb," Ria invited.

Eeva and Sawyer stepped to one side to let him in while Ria took Sol's hand and led the way.

Sawyer met Eeva's eyes after she'd shut the door behind their visitor. "What…?" he whispered.

Eeva shrugged then shook her head. "I have no idea," she murmured back.

CHAPTER 25

Evergreen sat beside her mother at the dining room table. Sawyer was at the end, on Evergreen's other side. Caleb sat across from Ria.

"Is black tea all right?" Ria asked.

"Yes, thank you for asking. Some of my faith do not drink caffeine, but I find I'm all right if it's occasionally and in moderation."

Ria smiled. "The middle way is often the best choice, I find. And I always ask. Running a retreat center, we encounter quite a few people with dietary restrictions."

"It's a beautiful lodge," Caleb complimented. "How long have you been running the center?"

"Oh, let me think. Eeva is twenty-two now, and we moved in when she was around a year old. Twenty-one years. Wow, I hadn't realized it had been that long. How long have you been in town?"

"About a month. I moved here for work," he said.

"Are you liking Birchland so far?"

"Yes, the people at the Kingdom Hall are very welcoming."

Ria nodded. "I'm glad to hear it."

"This is my first time out spreading the Word in Birchland. You're the first people willing to listen."

"Well, I enjoy learning other people's perspectives," Ria said.

"I noticed your home is decorated with a lot of greenery. Do you know what Christmas trees, gift-giving, and merry making have to do with the birth of our lord Jesus Christ?"

Evergreen exchanged a glance with Sawyer.

"I couldn't say," Ria answered.

"Nothing. All those things have absolutely nothing to do with his birth. Those are *Pagan* traditions. They stem from an ancient Roman holiday known as Saturnalia," Caleb proclaimed. "Jesus wasn't even born in December. That date was chosen to Christianize the festivals surrounding the winter solstice."

"I do know that, yes," Ria replied.

"The Bible tells us that only Christ's death should be commemorated."

"Jehovah's Witnesses celebrate Easter?" Evergreen asked, curious at the contradiction.

Caleb shook his head. "No, that too has Pagan origins. Rabbits and eggs? Those are symbols of false gods, of Pagan celebrations of fertility and spring. No, we commemorate the Memorial of Christ's Death."

Evergreen raised her eyebrows and blinked. "Well, that actually makes a lot of sense."

Caleb looked at each of them in turn. "This is not new information to you," he said, his eyebrows scrunching.

"That's not true," Evergreen countered. "I didn't know you have a holiday for Jesus's death."

"But everything else… You know of Christmas's Pagan origins, but you still celebrate it."

The idea seemed to baffle him as if just knowing the information would bring them to his way of seeing.

"Well, not exactly," Ria answered. "You see, we agree with you. We just—"

Ria's explanation was interrupted as Wes burst into the dining room. "Honey, look! It finally came in the mail. And just in time for Yule, too."

Wes wore a red cloak, its edges embroidered with golden Celtic knotwork. As he spun his back to them, he showed off the huge gold pentacle emblazoned on the back.

"Cool, right?" he said, turning back to them with a grin. "Oh, we have company. Sorry to interrupt. I was just excited. Hi, I'm Wes." He held out his hand to Caleb.

Caleb's eyes were wide, and his mouth hung open. He closed it and opened it again like a fish gasping for water. He took Wes's hand by reflex. "Caleb," he murmured like the wind had been knocked out of him.

"Welcome, Caleb." Wes turned his attention to Ria. "What were you guys talking about?"

"Oh, uh, I was just leaving actually. I have other people to visit, you see."

Evergreen tried to stifle a laugh but ended up snorting.

"It was nice to meet you all. Thank you for the tea." Caleb made a hasty retreat.

As soon as he was out of sight, Evergreen burst into laughter. "Oh my gods! Did you see his face? Dad, your timing was epic."

"Evergreen," Ria scolded. "Don't be unkind."

"Oh, come on, Mom. It was funny. They would like nothing better than to convert us. I mean, they love their martyrs, people who died refusing to give up their faith. But what do they do? They're out there trying to take faith from others, trying to take our gods, without a second thought. So what if I laughed a little at his reaction to finding out that the Big Bad Pagans are still alive and well."

"That's not how we educate people, Evergreen. That's not how we find common ground and understanding," her mother lectured.

"Yeah, well. You have your way. But this is my way of coping with the fact that we are *never* going to understand each other."

"That's just not true. You just told Caleb that you understood why Jehovah's Witnesses don't celebrate Christmas and Easter," Ria pointed out.

Evergreen frowned. "Yeah, but with the same information he went a completely different direction. I mean, he says these holidays are Pagan, so you shouldn't celebrate them. And we're like, yay Pagan holidays are still being celebrated."

Ria gave Evergreen a stern look, one she felt more than saw. "You wouldn't like it if people laughed at you for your beliefs, Evergreen Pendre."

Evergreen sighed. "No, I wouldn't."

"What is the Rede?"

Evergreen rolled her eyes. "Yeah, yeah. I got it."

"No, I want you to say it."

Evergreen groaned. "An' it harm none, do what ye will," she muttered.

"Good." Ria nodded with satisfaction. "Now, come here."

Evergreen plopped her head onto her mother's shoulder as Ria embraced her. Her irritation slid away the longer her mother patted her head.

"There is too much hate in the world already," Ria murmured. "We need to be better."

"I know. I'm sorry."

After releasing Evergreen, Ria stood from the table and took her and Caleb's cups to the kitchen.

Sawyer leaned toward Evergreen, resting his elbow on the table and cupping one hand around his mouth. "It was funny though," he whispered to her.

Evergreen snickered under her breath. "Right?"

CHAPTER 26

It was shortly before lunch, while Wes was chopping up fruit and setting deli meats and cheeses out on the island that utter chaos descended on the retreat center. The others began to arrive.

Piper rang the bell first, and Sawyer happened to be closest to the door at the time. As he opened it, he looked down at the petite woman buried deep in her winter things, only her light grey eyes peeking out from her hood and scarf.

"Piper? Is that you in there?" Sawyer asked.

The hood bobbed in assent.

Sawyer stepped aside so she could enter. As soon as the door was closed, Piper pulled the scarf from her face, sputtering as she tried to get the fuzzies off her lips.

"It's cold out there!" she complained. Then, she turned back to Sawyer and looked up at him. He was over a foot taller than her and nearly twice as wide. She leaned back as though he were a giant.

"What the heck are they feeding you? When did you get so huge?" she asked.

"You know, that's exactly what I said to Tara when I saw him, too," Ria said, coming to see who had arrived.

"Ria!" Piper grinned as she held out her arms to the woman. "It's been too long."

Ria agreed and embraced her.

"Don't you have any bags?" Ria asked.

Piper pulled off her hood, revealing her pixie-cut, white hair. "I do, but I left them in the car. The heater is broken, so I thought I'd come in and warm up first."

"I can go grab them for you," Sawyer offered.

"Oh, no. It's fine. There's too much." She waved her delicate hand.

"It's no problem," he insisted.

"I'll have Eeva and Cassandra help, too," Ria said.

The cousins came when they were called, and the three of them carried Piper's things into a room on the second floor.

Eeva shook her head as they placed Piper's luggage at the foot of the bed. "I will never understand how someone as small as Piper can snore so loudly."

Cassandra laughed. "Remember the first time we all went camping, and I told you it was a bear?"

"Remember? I didn't sleep the whole weekend!"

"Sometimes, you're too easy, cuz."

"I don't remember that," Sawyer said as they walked down the stairs.

"You and your mom hadn't moved here yet," Eeva explained.

Sawyer had only just bitten into his sandwich when the doorbell rang again.

Cassandra, who was putting a glass of milk in front of Sol, told everyone she would get it.

A few minutes later, she reappeared, a woman with frizzy, curly, black hair streaked with grey following her.

"Look who it is," Cassandra announced.

"Grandma!" Sol squealed and raced to hug the woman, who reacted with equal enthusiasm.

Morrigan embraced Ria next. "Little sister," she murmured. "Sorry I'm late."

"Oh, don't worry about it. We know you work crazy hours at the hospital."

"Hello, dear heart," Morrigan greeted as she kissed the top of Eeva's head. "How's school?"

"Well, I thought I was about to start my last semester, but… I'll tell you about it later."

Morrigan chuckled. "All right."

"I put you on the second floor with Cassandra and Sol," Ria told her sister.

Morrigan nodded. "Cassandra, would you take my things upstairs while I catch up with my favorite grandson?"

"I'm your *only* grandson," Sol pointed out.

Morrigan blinked. "Are you? Are you sure we haven't misplaced a brother anywhere?" She looked around as if she was really searching for another child.

Sol giggled. "You're silly, Grandma."

Morrigan ruffled the boy's hair as Cassandra left to take up her things.

Devan arrived next, his booming voice carrying to the sitting room as he greeted Eeva at the door.

"Am I the last?" he asked.

"Not this time," Eeva said, leading him into the room where the others were catching up.

Devan was not a tall man, and he was stouter than Sawyer remembered. But he still had the same chin-length pale hair and the same well-trimmed goatee. He smiled his greeting at everyone. "You all thought I would be late? Didn't you?" he challenged.

"There's a first time for everything," Wes teased.

"Devan, you're in the attic. I hope that's okay," Ria told him.

"No problem at all." He patted his belly. "I could use the exercise," he declared with a chuckle.

Cassandra and Eeva carried his bag and CPAP machine upstairs for him.

It was still early afternoon when Dorian and Cory arrived.

"Can I get some help?" Cassandra called from the front door.

Sawyer and Eeva rose to assist her, realizing why she'd asked when they arrived.

Cory, a six-foot-three, ripped beast of a man, stood just inside, his foot in a splint and crutches under his arms.

Meanwhile, his husband, Dorian, held a car seat in one hand and a teddy bear in the other. He had diaper bags crisscrossed over his chest.

"What happened?" Eeva asked, staring at Cory's foot.

"Oh, don't even ask," Dorian said. "He'll give you the whole play-by-play. Short version: he got hurt playing hockey."

"Is it broken?" Sawyer asked.

"It's only sprained. Don't let him whine too much about it," Dorian advised.

"And who is this?" Cassandra asked, tilting her head at the car seat.

"Let's get inside, and we'll introduce you," Cory said.

Once Cory was seated comfortably in an armchair, his foot propped up on the ottoman, Dorian took the blanket off the car seat.

"Everyone," Dorian said, unbuckling the baby inside, "We'd like you to meet Ella."

The baby girl couldn't have been more than six months old. She looked around at them, her eyes big and blue under a mess of strawberry blonde hair.

"Hi, Ella," Eeva cooed, smiling at the baby. "Aw, look at her cute little frilly dress."

"I picked it out," Cory said proudly.

"The adoption went through last month," Dorian informed. "It has been an adjustment, but we're finally getting the hang of it."

"Don't you worry," Ria said. "We've got the crib all set up for you."

"Mom, you knew? Why didn't you say?" Eeva complained.

"Well, they wanted it to be a surprise, and they couldn't very well not tell me to prepare for a baby in the house."

"Can I hold her?" Eeva asked.

"Sure," Dorian said. "After you wash your hands."

"Okay." Eeva went and washed her hands then sat on the couch, where Dorian handed her the baby. "Hello, Ella. Pretty girl. I'm so glad you've come to visit us. I bet you like being adopted by your daddies. You don't worry one bit. They're going to take good care of you."

Sawyer sat beside her on the couch, looking over at Eeva

and Ella gazing at each other. His chest warmed, and he smiled gently.

Muir jumped up on the couch between Eeva and Sawyer, wanting to see what the commotion was about. He looked at Ella, and Ella looked at him. Then he started to meow, loud and insistent.

Eeva chuckled. "Here," she said to Dorian, holding Ella out to him. "Muir doesn't seem to like the competition."

After Ella had been passed back, Eeva picked up Muir and held him like a baby, stroking his chest and belly. "I know. I know. I'm a traitor," she murmured to the cat.

Muir purred and closed his eyes.

Just as Wes was finishing dinner and the whole house smelled of slow cooked pot roast, the last of the old coven arrived.

Eeva led Hazel into the dining room. She hadn't changed at all since they'd seen her last. She was still reedy with long, dark hair and flowing garments of varying shades of blue.

"Sorry I'm late," Hazel apologized. "Charlie was being a handful. How that man is going to survive without me for the next ten days I have no idea." She glanced around at everyone, her gaze landing on Devan. "What? Even Devan got here before me."

Everyone chuckled and sat down to eat.

CHAPTER 27

*L*ater that evening, everyone sat in the common room knitting, quilting, and just catching up. Devan, who lay on the floor near the fire, asked, "When was the last time we were all together like this?"

"Eeva's dedication," Piper answered, her memory as sharp as ever.

"That was just before Sawyer went off to college," Tara said.

"Yeah, the summer before," Cory agreed. "Because there was that huge storm the night before."

Everyone fell into a thoughtful silence, one blurry with memories.

Evergreen remembered that night, the most important night thus far on her Pagan path. Cory was right. It had stormed the night before. She recalled that the path beneath her bare feet had still been wet.

Though they had always referred to themselves as a coven, that wasn't strictly accurate. Unlike an actual coven, there was no lineage, no passing of secret truths. They were just a group of eclectic Pagans who celebrated the sabbats and esbats together. They were a group of like-minded friends who performed magic together more than anything. And so, there was no initiation to be had.

Still, they did have a tradition for dedication, a practice usually reserved for solitary practitioners. The group saw their relationships with deity as unique and individual. So, when Evergreen felt she was old enough to declare that she would continue on this spiritual path, she asked to have a dedication ceremony.

The coven was there only to show support. They were there on the patio in full regalia, ready to send her on her journey. Her father gave her the lantern that would light her way, and her mother took her cloak so she could meet the gods in the same state as she'd been born.

She walked down the soggy dirt path through the woods, mud squelching between her toes. When she reached the clearing, she performed her ritual, swearing to all who would listen that she dedicated herself to the old ways, that she would honor and celebrate the Earth and its seasons, that she would endeavor to live in perfect love and perfect trust.

When she returned to the coven, still waiting on the patio, her cloak was returned, and they all had a big party.

"I've got an idea," Piper said, pulling Evergreen from her memories. "That is, if you guys want to, of course. Why don't we have a naming ceremony for little Ella?"

Cory and Dorian exchanged looks then Dorian nodded. "That's a wonderful idea, Piper. But will we have time? I mean, we're already preparing for Yule."

"Oh, don't worry about that," Ria assured, looking down at the baby in her arms. "We've got most of what we need already. And what's most important is that we're all together. Isn't that right, baby Ella?"

"We should all go into town tomorrow," Cassandra suggested. "Then we can shop for Yule gifts and naming gifts for baby Ella. We can have the naming ceremony the day after."

Everyone agreed to the prospect with enthusiasm.

As Ria handed Ella to Cory, Evergreen could hear the dreamy smile in her voice when she said, "I can't wait to be a grandma."

"You're hurting Muir's feelings," Evergreen chided, putting her free hand over the cat's ears.

It wasn't long before Evergreen called it a night. The day had been full, and she wanted to be asleep well before Sawyer crawled into the sleeping bag beside her.

But such was not her luck. She was still staring up at the glass ceiling when he came into the meditation room.

He crept in, trying not to wake her. She could hear him suppressing his breathing.

"I'm awake," she told him.

"Oh, okay," he murmured, letting out a sigh. He turned on the dim yellow lamp in the corner.

As a heavy silence choked the room, Evergreen wished she hadn't said anything.

"Do you…need me to leave so you can change into your pajamas?" she asked softly.

"No, it's fine. I'll just change in the bathroom when it's free."

She watched as he dug through his bag. "You could just

change in the corner. I mean, you're wearing underwear, aren't you? I won't peep."

His eyes slid over to hers. "I'm not shy," he told her.

"Neither am I," she stated. "But it would be rude to look without permission."

His gaze was level and serious, and she could feel him analyzing her response to what he was about to ask. "Is that something…you want? Permission, that is."

Evergreen imagined Sawyer slowly unbuttoning his jeans. *Yes,* she thought. "No, that's not what I meant. I was speaking generally," she said.

"Because…" Sawyer continued softly. "You can if you want… I wouldn't mind."

Evergreen's heart leapt into her throat. She turned on her side, facing the glass wall. "I didn't say that," she murmured. "I was only trying to make things more convenient for you. Take it or leave it. I don't care." But her voice sounded a little too uneven to be convincing.

"All right," he conceded. "I will then."

"Fine. Go ahead."

The night was dark outside the glass, and the lamp cast reflections. Evergreen watched, her eyes drawn to the movement. And though her vision didn't permit her to see anything in detail, she saw enough for her mind to wander back to her dream from the night before. A dull ache arose in her core, and she clenched her jaw.

Sawyer turned off the lamp, his now-fully-clothed reflection disappearing into the night. Evergreen sighed, hoping its retreat would make her desire wane. But as Sawyer climbed into his sleeping bag on the floor beside her, she could feel his presence behind her, his solid, warm presence. He didn't touch her, didn't even reach for her. But her skin started to tingle as if anticipating his caress.

She adjusted to lay on her back, taking a deep breath and letting it out all at once. *This is going to be a rough night,* she thought. Acknowledging her desire for Sawyer had done nothing to alleviate the feeling. In fact, if anything, it had made it worse.

Bury it, Evergreen, she told herself. *There's no relief in sight, so just bury it.*

"Are you warm enough?" Sawyer asked, his voice soft and way closer than she'd expected. "I can switch places with you if you'd like to be closer to the heater."

"I'm fine," she muttered.

She stared up at the ceiling, trying to concentrate on the clouds overhead, trying to push her body's sensations out of her.

"About what your mom said before," he started. "Does she bug you a lot about having grandchildren? My mom does."

Evergreen latched onto the conversation, anything to distract herself. "No, not really. I mean, I know she wants to be a grandma, but it's not like she pressures me or anything."

"Do you…want to have kids?"

Evergreen sighed, her desire slipping out of her under the weight of the topic. "Sure. But, you know, it's not that simple for me."

"Why not?"

"Well, my eye disease is genetic. That means my children would have a greater chance of having it, too. At the very least, they all would be carriers. And can I be an effective parent without being able to see? I mean, I couldn't even take my kids to school. I couldn't even drive them to the hospital if they were sick or hurt."

Evergreen heard Sawyer turn toward her, but she didn't look over at him.

"Would you have not wanted to be born?" he asked softly.

"What do you mean?"

"I mean, if your parents had known you would be blind, if you could make that decision, would you still want to be born?"

"Of course I would. Even a life with blindness is better than no life. But just because I feel that way doesn't mean my kids will. And I know better than anyone the struggles they will face."

"And you will be able to teach them how to face them better than anyone. And let me add that it's total nonsense that you couldn't be an effective parent. That's bullshit. You've found ways to adapt to every situation. You're telling me you couldn't adapt to motherhood? You're the strongest, most competent person I know. If you decided to be a mother, I know you'll be amazing at it, just like you're amazing at everything else. I mean, you're so good. You make it look easy, effortless."

"It's not though. It's hard work."

"I know. And you don't shy away from that work either. I think society needs more parents like you. You know…not to influence your decision or anything."

Warmth spread through Evergreen's chest, and with it, light and contentment and…*hope?* She didn't dare look over at Sawyer, afraid of what her expression might say. "Thank you," she murmured.

"Anytime." Sawyer paused for a moment. "We've known

each other a long time, but I don't think I've ever heard you say. Do you mind if I ask you what your eyesight is like?"

The question she'd been asked so many times put her back in comfortable territory. "I don't mind, though I've had bad vision my whole life so I don't know how much sense my explanation will make. I don't have anything to compare it to."

"That's fine."

"I think of my vision like impressionist art. Maybe sighted people see the world like a realist painting, but my vision is a lot of guesswork. For example, if I see a round circle on a wall above a door. It's white with a dark edge. I assume it's a clock. I can't read the numbers or see the hands, but it's a safe bet it's a clock. It could not be a clock. It could be a barometric pressure gauge for all I know. I can see someone sitting across the table from me, but I can't necessarily see his or her facial expressions because facial expressions are often too minute. So I rely on how people sound when they speak, or don't speak for that matter. And I sort of feel the vibes coming off them if that makes sense. I can do a lot of things by touch, like knitting for instance. Sometimes I run into things as I'm not great at judging distance, or maybe that's just my excuse for being clumsy. I'm also color deficient, meaning I can't always tell colors that are close in shade. I might call something green when it's yellow. It's easier if I can compare them side by side. Contrast is easier, especially if the background is vastly different from an object. I'm also light sensitive, and lighting can vastly impact what I can see in any given situation. Does that help you understand better?"

"Yeah. Thanks for sharing that with me."

"No problem."

CHAPTER 28

When Sawyer awoke the next morning, Eeva was no longer in her sleeping bag beside him. The thick scent of cinnamon hung in the air, and the candles on the altar were lit, telling him she had already been busy that morning.

Once he'd changed, he went out to see who all was up and about. Eeva was in the common room with Hazel and Cory. Eeva and Hazel cradled mugs in their hands, their feet tucked under them on the couch. They watched Cory talk to Ella as he fed her.

"So, what do you say, Eeva?" Dorian asked, entering the room, a steaming cup in each hand. "You know how it's done, and Cory isn't exactly up for it this year."

"Sure," Eeva agreed with a nod. "I have no problem. And I know you'll teach me anything I forgot. We have time to practice, right?"

"Oh, honey, I can't do it either. Cory is going to have a hard enough time just getting around himself. I have to help him and watch baby Ella."

"Why not Sawyer?" Hazel suggested. "He did it that one year, didn't he?"

They all turned their attention to Sawyer, who covered his mouth as he yawned. He hadn't gotten a lot of sleep the night before, too aware of Eeva beside him. "I what now?"

"You know the dance. You could play the oak king. Couldn't you?" Hazel asked.

"Oh, yeah. I mean, it has been a while, but sure."

"Great," Dorian said with a smile. "Then Eeva can be our holly king, and Sawyer can be our oak king. Don't forget to practice, you two."

Sawyer glanced at Eeva. She did not look as happy at the prospect as she had a few moments before. *Maybe I misread her,* he thought. *Maybe that whole kiss thing was just a fluke. I mean, surely the thought of partnering with me wouldn't be that upsetting if she felt something for me...anything... Should I back off? I feel like I was pretty up-front last night. Maybe I should just tell her outright instead of leading up to it. Maybe I should just tell her how I feel... But if she isn't ready to hear it, it may not end the way I want. Timing is everything.*

Once everyone else was awake and had breakfasted, Wes announced that he would be staying home while they went shopping.

"I've got to make the cakes and ale for the naming ceremony," he explained.

"What will you be making?" Piper asked.

"I'm thinking about crescent moon cutout cookies and faux

mead. You know, since I won't have time to ferment actual mead."

"Okay, the kitchen witch will stay home to do his brewing," Morrigan acknowledged.

"I'm staying, too," Cory said. "I don't want to tempt falling on the ice. Ella and I can stay here with Wes. It's too cold to take her out for too long anyway." He smiled at Dorian, leaning over and kissing his cheek. "You go have fun. We'll be fine here with Wes."

Everyone else split into three cars and headed for town. Most of Birchland's shops were situated near each other in the shopping district, so they just parked along the side of the road and bundled in their winter things to walk.

The first shop they went to was Toil and Trouble, the Pagan supply store and new age shop. In the front window was a set of shelves, which held crystal balls, statues of gods and goddesses, wands, and a carved dragon that clung to the front as if scaling it. The dragon wore a tiny Santa hat. A sign in the window informed that tarot card readings were available by appointment.

The air inside Toil and Trouble was thick with the heady smell of dragon's blood incense.

The shopkeeper looked up as they all shuffled in. "Ria," the young woman greeted. "Good to see you. And I see you've brought guests."

Ria smiled. "Yes, this is most of my old coven. They all moved away before you opened the shop. Guys, this is Clover. This shop is her labor of love."

"It's lovely," Hazel complimented.

"Thank you," Clover said. "Go ahead and take a look around. Let me know if you have any questions."

Everyone acknowledged and squeezed into the space.

Sawyer was surprised to find that they had quite a few baby things. He decided to get Ella a onesie with a buckler on the front that said "Shield Maiden."

Sawyer found Eeva's green head easily across the room. She was bent over a glass case with jewelry in it. He perused the shelves, thinking of all the Yules they'd missed together. *Should I get her something again this year?* he wondered. But he knew he still had Yule gifts from the past four Yules in his bag in the meditation room. *Maybe I should just give her the gifts I've been saving. It may be a little weird to give her five gifts after all.*

He stopped in front of a shelf, a glint of light reflecting off faceted glass catching his eye. Before him was a shelf full of glass figurines. A stick with mistletoe, bright green with white berries on top stood in a mosaic cup.

He reached out and pulled the smooth stick from the cup. He'd thought it was glass, but it felt more like plastic.

"It's resin," Clover told him, appearing beside him as he examined it. "It's real mistletoe. I harvested it myself and preserved it in resin to make the hair pin. Pretty, isn't it?"

Sawyer nodded.

"How long are we going to be here?" Sol whined to his mother further down the aisle. He pulled on her hand in emphasis.

"Be patient, Sol," Cassandra told him.

Sawyer approached them. "I'm pretty much done here, Cassandra. I can keep Sol occupied if you need more time," he offered.

"Oh gods, would you?" she asked.

Sawyer knelt down to the boy. "What do you say, my friend? Do you want to go on a quest?"

"A quest? What's that?"

"It's a journey where a brave warrior goes in search of something."

"What are we going to search for?"

Sawyer grinned. "For ice cream, of course. What other kind of quest is there?"

Sol's eyes lit up at the prospect. "What about Eeva? Can Eeva come too?"

"Sure she can," Sawyer agreed. "I'm just going to go buy these things. Why don't you ask Eeva if she wants to come on our quest?"

"Okay!"

Sawyer went to the cash register and purchased the onesie and the hair pin. By the time they were carefully wrapped, Sol and Eeva had reached him.

"You ready?" he asked them.

"You two can head outside. I just have a few purchases to make real quick," Eeva said.

Sawyer nodded, glancing at her hands to see what she was buying. She didn't have anything.

"We're on a quest for ice cream, a quest for ice cream!" Sol cheered as they headed for the door.

CHAPTER 29

Evergreen thanked Clover as she handed her the paper bag with her purchases. She smiled to herself, warmth blooming in her chest. *It's perfect,* she thought. *Just the right size and color.*

She zipped up her winter coat and left Toil and Trouble. Sawyer and Sol were waiting for her outside on the sidewalk.

"Okay, I'm ready," she said.

"Witches! Heathens! You'll all burn in Hell!"

Evergreen's stomach jumped into her throat as a man, who seemed to just have been passing them on the sidewalk, began to yell at them.

She turned her back to ignore him; she had long discovered that arguing with his type wasn't worth it.

"Don't turn your back on me, you whore of Satan," he sneered.

Evergreen's heart pounded as fear crept across her skin. She looked down at Sol; his eyes were wide and afraid. Anger churned in her stomach. She took his hand and rounded on their assaulter.

"You don't need to do this," she told him, hoping he couldn't hear the quiver in her voice. "Can't you see you're frightening this child?"

"He should be afraid. The fires of Hell will burn his flesh and melt his soul with eternal torment. He even wears the mark of the Devil," the man spat, pointing at the pentacle on Sol's chest.

"Eeva," Sol murmured, tugging on her hand.

She knelt down to see him better. Tears streaked down his cheeks.

"Why is he yelling at us?" he asked.

Evergreen wrapped her arms around Sol, not having the words to explain to him at the moment.

The man was blocked from her view as Sawyer stepped in between them. "I think you need to leave," he said, his voice low, his threat clear.

"'Blessed are those who are persecuted for righteousness' sake, for theirs is the kingdom of Heaven. Blessed are you when others revile you and persecute you and utter all kinds of evil against you falsely on my account. Rejoice and be glad, for your reward is great in Heaven, for so they persecuted the prophets, who were before y—'"

"Daniel!" a woman scolded, firmly interrupting the man.

Evergreen peeked around Sawyer to see a short, round woman stomping toward them.

"Please, tell me you aren't harassing these nice people. We talked about this. You can't keep doing this," she censured.

"I have the freedom of speech. This is America!" the man shouted at her.

"Yeah, and that same amendment gives them the freedom of religion."

"A man or a woman who is a medium or deals with the spirits of the dead must certainly be put to death. They must be stoned to death. Their blood is on them," he countered.

"Really? Death threats now? You know, Daniel, one of these days you're going to be charged with a hate crime."

"We live in a Christian nation. Our leaders will see the righteousness of my words."

"That's enough," the woman said finally. "We can talk about this at home. Go wait in the car."

"Woman—"

"Don't you 'woman' me. Go."

The man squinted his hatred one more time before he stormed back the way he'd come. Then, the woman turned toward Sawyer, Evergreen, and Sol.

"I am so sorry," she apologized, her voice thick with regret. "There isn't any excuse I can give for my husband's behavior. He's on this new evangelical kick. I have no idea what has gotten into him. I hope he didn't scare you too much. Are you okay?"

Evergreen stood, lifting Sol in her arms. Sawyer looked over at her as she moved to stand beside him. She could feel his gaze on her face, analyzing her emotional state.

"I think we're all right. It may take us just a bit to calm down," he told her.

"Well…I hope you know that all Christians aren't like that. Some of us are very accepting. Just… You have allies amongst us. Though I'm sure that doesn't mean much to you at the moment."

"That's not true," Evergreen told her. "It's a relief to have a Christian stand up to one of their own, to hold them accountable for that behavior. We're shaken up, but I'm grateful you stepped in."

The woman smiled, and even Evergreen could see the light shining from her face. "Thank you, and I'm sorry again. I hope you three have a very happy solstice. You look like such a nice family."

"Thank you, and merry Christmas to you," Sawyer said.

"Merry Christmas," Evergreen seconded as the woman nodded and followed her husband.

Evergreen heaved a deep sigh, trying to steady her still-racing heart.

"Are you all right?" Sawyer asked.

She swallowed and gave him a small nod. "I'm okay."

"How about you, my friend? Are you okay?" Sawyer asked, rubbing Sol's shoulder.

"Was that man going to hurt us?" Sol asked.

Sawyer frowned. "It's hard to say," he told the boy honestly. "But you better believe that Eeva and I would never let anyone hurt you. Okay?"

Sol nodded.

"Do you still want to go on that quest for ice cream? Or do you want us to take you inside to your mom and grandma?" Sawyer asked him.

"I want strawberry," Sol declared. "No, I want chocolate."

"Why don't we get both strawberry *and* chocolate?" Sawyer asked.

Sol squirmed in Evergreen's arms, and she put him down.

"Yeah!" he agreed.

His enthusiasm, his child's way of pushing the bad experience aside, of living in the moment made Evergreen's anxiety slip away.

"We're on a quest for ice cream, a quest for ice cream," Sol sang, holding out a hand to Evergreen and Sawyer in turn.

And as they all walked hand-in-hand, Evergreen remembered the woman saying how they looked like a family. She glanced sidelong at Sawyer. She couldn't see him well from this distance, but she just knew he was smiling. Warmth spread through Evergreen's chest, and with it returned the light and contentment from the night before. And, yes, she recognized it now. It was hope. The world paused for just a second as if her heart had taken a picture of the moment.

CHAPTER 30

Sawyer let his sigh out slowly so as not to wake Eeva as she lay beside him. He'd presented a strong front that afternoon, but if he was being honest with himself, the encounter outside Toil and Trouble had frightened him. Not because he thought the man would hurt them. No, he knew he could protect Eeva and Sol. He was afraid at the sheer magnitude of his anger. He would not have hesitated in striking that man down had he made a move toward Eeva or Sol. The image of Eeva's pale face as she clutched the crying child to her, her quivering voice as she'd challenged the man, his blood still boiled to think of it. He'd never been so angry in his life, and it left the taste of shame behind.

And for the rest of the day, Eeva had been quiet. He hadn't felt much from her. She seemed still, contemplative. And when she'd looked at him—and he'd caught her doing so quite a few times—her gaze had been open as if she were asking him a question he couldn't understand.

Sawyer lay on his side, watching Eeva's tranquil face as she slept. Muir lay between them on her sleeping bag, unconsciously purring in contentment, Eeva's hand was buried in his fur. Sawyer reached out hesitantly, holding his breath as his heart picked up speed. He stroked Muir, his fingers millimeters from Eeva's. He pulled back before he woke her and closed his eyes. Listening to her slow, even breathing, he matched his rhythm with hers and drifted off to sleep.

The next day was a flurry of activity at the retreat center. Some were getting things ready for the naming ceremony that evening, while others were playing games or doing crafts. Morrigan was looking everywhere for something she'd misplaced—swearing that the faeries had hid it because she hadn't left them a gift, which was her custom. Ria had taken over the meditation room so she could perform reiki on Cory. Piper was drawing up Tara's star chart for the coming year, and Hazel and Devan were facing off in an intense game of weiqi.

Sawyer found Eeva in the kitchen, helping her dad frost the moon cookies he'd made the day before.

"Hey, Eeva. You mentioned yesterday that you wanted to practice the holly king versus the oak king before Yule. We can do that when you're done if you want," Sawyer said.

"Oh, I can handle things here," Wes assured. "Eeva, go on ahead and practice with Sawyer."

"But Mom is using the meditation room," Eeva said. "Where are we going to practice?"

"Just go out to the patio," Wes suggested. "I'm sure you'll warm up once you start moving around."

"All right." Eeva nodded and stuck the tip of her finger in

her mouth, removing the smear of yellow frosting. "Where are the practice staves?"

"In the garage," Wes answered.

She nodded. "Meet you outside in a sec," she told Sawyer.

He acknowledged and went to put his coat on over his hoodie.

Eeva joined Sawyer outside shortly, a staff in each hand. She offered him one, and he took it.

"Do you remember the steps?" he asked.

"Vaguely. As I recall they're fairly simple. It's the feeling, the rhythm that's more important."

Sawyer nodded. "Right. And since this is the winter solstice and you're playing the holly king, you're the one who loses this time."

"Yeah, okay. Let's give it a try. You got a beat?"

"Sure, I'll use the one I used to practice before. But of course, it'll be different the day of since the drum circle will be going."

Sawyer pressed play on his cellphone, and the sound of drums started from the speaker as "Punagra" played. He put it on repeat and placed the phone on the step. He faced Eeva, loosening his shoulders to the primal beat.

As Eeva shifted her weight from foot to foot, swaying in time, they started the simple steps of the dance, circling each other.

"Yeah, that's it," Sawyer encouraged. "You remember. Ready for the staff?"

Eeva smiled. "Go for it."

Sawyer struck out with his staff, and Eeva met it with hers.

He did it again with the same result. And so they went on in rhythm, the mock battle playing out in a dance. They circled each other. They clashed in the middle. They retreated.

Sawyer's heart raced as the exercise made him warm in his coat. He took it off, his steps still in time. Eeva did the same, her breaths punctuated by white puffs from her lips.

"Ready to try the end?" Sawyer asked her.

"Come at me," she challenged, her voice teasing.

Sawyer attacked, bringing his face in close to hers, their staves crossed between them. This was where he was supposed to push them apart. She was to fall to the ground, defeated. But as they locked eyes, and he felt her breath on his face, they both froze.

The music played on in the background but seemed very far away. And there it was again, the look that beckoned him. Eeva's eyes were deep and serious, and they were trained on him. This time, he didn't speak. He didn't want the sound of his voice to pull her from the moment. Still, as he leaned down toward her, he did so slowly, giving her time to retreat.

Just as he felt her warm breath on his mouth, he looked at her through heavy eyelids. Her eyes were lightly shut. He smiled then pressed his lips to hers. The kiss was soft and sweet. And though lust pumped in his veins, he reined it in, focusing on the pleasant ache in his chest. He broke the kiss but didn't pull away.

As Eeva's clouded blue eyes met his, her face flushed. He smiled gently at her. *It has finally happened,* he thought. *I did it. Surely she knows how I feel now. And she didn't resist either. She kissed me back.* Sawyer's head was fuzzy with giddiness.

"Um… Can we practice another time?" Eeva asked softly. "I think I need a minute."

Sawyer sobered, trying to quiet his inner cheers of triumph. *This is coming out of nowhere for her,* he thought. *Of course she needs time to process.* "Sure, no problem," he told her.

CHAPTER 31

*E*vergreen nodded slowly. Then, she leaned her staff against the side of the house and grabbed her coat. Too warm still to put it on, she folded it over her arm and started down the path through the woods.

What...? What...? What the hell was that? she thought. Her heart pounded in her fingertips, and her crunching footsteps sounded very loud in her ears.

She halted on the path, her breaths long and deep. "We kissed," she murmured. She closed her eyes. She could still feel Sawyer's lips on hers like the far away echo of a low and sweet melody.

Evergreen grinned, her entire body tingling as if she were having a pleasant panic attack. "We kissed," she breathed, soft and happy.

But her joy was short lived. Reality descended upon her, and her stomach dropped as the smile slid from her face. "We kissed," she said again, dread coloring her tone.

What does this mean? she wondered. *Why would he kiss me? I mean, other than he felt like it. Did he just feel like it? Is it that simple?*

She thought back to his reaction after he'd pulled away. *No, that can't be right. I felt...relief from him. Like he'd been holding it in for a long time. Could I have misread him all along?*

Evergreen shook her head. *No, that can't be true either. If he'd been harboring feelings for me for that long, he would have stayed in touch. Right? I wouldn't have been...so easy to forget.*

She tried to swallow the lump that rose in her throat. *It doesn't matter,* she thought. *That's not the question here. Why would he kiss me? And why would he feel relieved afterward? Maybe he was just relieved I didn't pull away like last time. Yeah, that makes sense. But what does that mean for what comes next?*

She couldn't lie to herself about how it had felt. It had been everything she'd wished for before. How many times had she prayed, begged in her mind for Sawyer to lean just a little farther down, to give her some indication that he wanted her as much as she wanted him?

But he never had. He had always been so calm and balanced. Nothing phased him. It was one of the things she'd loved about him. He never wasted words. But he always had an answer, a solution to whatever situation that had fired her up. She'd liked to think he cared in a quiet sort of way, like the base of a pillar. It doesn't draw as much attention, but it's equally if not more important. That's how she'd always seen him, an ever-present, if silent, support.

Which of course is why I was so fucked up when he'd left, she thought. *He'd been a steadying presence, something to navigate by, and then he left and didn't look back.*

But, thinking about it now, he was always the still, silent reflection type. I was the one who jumped into action, with everything but love that is. When I look at it that way, it doesn't make sense that he would have made a move back then. So what's different now? Has he changed so much?

Evergreen thought about everything she'd witnessed over the last few days. *Yes, he has changed quite a bit. He never would have threatened that man before or confronted the woman at the craft store. He wouldn't have been so forceful about me not riding with Niko. And he obviously never kissed me, even when I wanted it so desperately. Even so, it's the little things that tell me he's still the Sawyer I knew: he remembered how I like my hot cocoa, he's still polite and considerate, he's sweet with Sol, and he helped me find a better way to approach my career.*

A gentle warmth settled into her heart, and she smiled at the familiar feeling. *He's different. Of course, he is. I am too. I don't know anything about his life right now, but I can learn. I want to learn.*

And though anxiety clenched her gut, Evergreen didn't allow it to take over. *Maybe this time it will work out. There's no ignoring this feeling anyway. I might as well make the best of it.*

Evergreen took a deep breath and headed back toward the house. She entered just as her dad called that lunch was ready.

The island was packed with taco stuff, and a queue had formed.

"Don't worry, Tara, Piper," Wes told the women as Evergreen took her place at the back of the line. "I made black beans for you since I know you're vegetarians."

"Are you sure I can't take this man off your hands?" Piper asked Ria.

"Go ahead and try. You'll give him back in a week. He's needy," Ria said affectionately, rubbing her husband's back.

"It's true," Wes agreed. "I'm like a puppy."

"You mean, you aren't house trained?" Devan asked.

Everyone laughed.

After Evergreen had gotten her tacos, she made her way to the dining room. The only free chair was between Morrigan and Piper, across from Sawyer. She sank into the seat, furtively glancing at him.

Their eyes met. He smiled. And as her cheeks heated, she smiled back.

A shiver ran down Evergreen's spine as Morrigan stroked her hair. Evergreen jumped as if caught doing something she wasn't supposed to.

"So, what's going on, Eeva? You mentioned something had changed with school?" Morrigan said.

"Oh, yeah. Well, I was having a hard time finding a job. You know I've always wanted to work in a museum."

Morrigan nodded.

"Well, Sawyer looked some stuff up for me, and he told me that you can get a certificate that really helps you get those jobs. Part of the program is that you have to have an internship. And it sounds like if you do really well, not only can you get a job at the museum after, but they might even pay for higher degrees."

"Wow, that's amazing. So, are you going to do it then?"

"I called the university and made an appointment with my academic adviser after the holidays."

"That's excellent. I hope it works out," Morrigan said.

"Yeah, me too," Evergreen agreed.

CHAPTER 32

The sun set early that evening, and the meditation room felt enchanted as the coven filed into the space under the watchful light of the waning gibbous. Devan had already cleansed the room, and everyone was smudged prior to entering. The sharp scent of white sage and the mellow saccharinity of sweetgrass still lingered in Sawyer's nose. He felt light, the burned herbs having blessed him and banished any negative energies. A reverent hush descended as Cory and Dorian carried their daughter into the room and toward the altar.

They turned and faced the coven, who had formed a circle. Everyone had changed into their best garments from cloaks to flowing dresses to jeans and sweaters. They wore them with purpose, which was what mattered.

"We gather on this night to ask and receive blessings for this child, to give her name power, and to introduce her to you and the gods," Cory declared, gesturing at Ella in Dorian's arms.

"Please face East," Cory said, turning in the correct direction.

"Spirits of the East, element of Air, please join our circle. Hail and welcome," Dorian said.

As Dorian spoke, Sawyer imagined the wind blowing the hair from his face and the sound of rustling leaves.

"Hail and welcome," everyone responded.

Cory lit the incense on the east side of the altar. Then, everyone turned South.

"Spirits of the South, element of Fire, please join our circle. Hail and welcome."

Sawyer's face was warmed by a visualized flame.

"Hail and welcome."

Cory lit the candle on the south end of the altar.

Everyone turned West, their hands raised as if to embrace each element.

"Spirits of the West, element of Water, please join our circle. Hail and welcome."

Sawyer imagined the feel of rain dripping down his face and neck.

"Hail and welcome."

Cory lifted the bowl of water from the west side of the altar, held it at head level, and nodded his head in a bow.

They all faced North.

"Spirits of the North, element of Earth, please join our circle. Hail and welcome."

Sawyer pictured the warm soil of spring and the scent of freshly cut grass.

"Hail and welcome."

Cory lifted the bowl of salt from the north side of the altar, held it at head level, and nodded his head in a bow.

Sawyer turned back toward the center of the circle as did the others. He placed his hands, one over the other, at the center of his chest and closed his eyes.

"Divine Spirit within, please join our circle. Hail and welcome."

He imagined a soft purple glow at the center of his chest.

"Hail and welcome."

"Goddess, Divine Mother, Sacred Sister, we invite you to join our circle. Hail and welcome."

"Hail and welcome."

Cory lit a candle to represent the goddess.

"God, Divine Father, Sacred Brother, we invite you to join our circle. Hail and welcome."

"Hail and welcome."

Cory lit the candle that represented the god. Then, he took the bottle Wes had filled with faux mead and poured it into a bowl between the goddess and god candles. "To the Lord and Lady," he declared. "Blessed be."

"Blessed be," they echoed.

"Before we finish casting our circle," Dorian said. "Let us raise energy with a chant."

The group listened as Dorian sang the chant and then joined in as he repeated it.

"Circle, circle, circle of light, protect us as we work this rite."

Sawyer lifted his voice in song, harmonizing with those around him. And as they repeated the chant over and over, his heart lightened, and the room seemed to hum with the energy they raised.

As the last note died away, Dorian turned to Ria and took her hand. "Ria, hand to hand I cast the circle."

Ria turned to Wes, who stood on her left. "Wesley, hand to hand I cast the circle."

And so it went on around the room until Cory turned to Dorian and said, "Dorian, hand to hand I cast the circle."

"The circle is cast," Dorian declared.

"Tonight, we stand at this altar, and ask that the gods, goddesses, spirits, and elements give us guidance on the path ahead," Cory said. "May we teach Ella all she needs to know to prepare for her to stand on her own, and may she ever have love and support when she needs it most."

Cory took the incense from the altar and turned to Dorian and Ella. He moved it in a circular motion so the incense wafted around her. "Spirits of Air, we ask that you bless Ella with curiosity and communication. May she be ever curious to learn new things and expand her knowledge. May her voice be strong and clear so she may never suffer in silence."

Cory replaced the incense on the altar and took the fire element candle. He carefully circled it around Ella. "Spirits of Fire, we ask that you bless Ella with protection, passion, and courage. May she have the passion to have dreams, the courage to follow them, and the protection that her feet may never fail her."

Cory replaced the candle on the altar and brought the bowl of water to his daughter. He dipped his fingers into the bowl and sprinkled the water onto her forehead. "Spirits of Water, we ask that you bless Ella with peace and compassion. May her heart have few troubles, and may her actions heal the troubles of others."

Cory replaced the water on the altar and took the bowl of salt. Taking a pinch, he sprinkled it over her head, carefully avoiding her eyes. "Spirit of Earth, we ask that you bless Ella with prosperity and conscientiousness. May she be a good steward of the planet and all the life it supports, and may her hard work be rewarded."

Cory returned the salt to the altar and faced the center of the circle. "We call on the ancestors to guide Ella as she learns and grows."

"We call on the Mother Goddess and the Father God to nurture and protect Ella as she walks her own path," Dorian said.

"If anyone would like to bestow blessings on Ella, please do so at this time."

Dorian presented Ella to Ria. "I would like to bestow the blessing of health and vitality on you, Ella," Ria said before kissing the baby's forehead.

Dorian presented Ella to Wes. "May your belly always be full and your heart big enough to share what you have with others," Wes said. Then he kissed Ella's forehead.

Dorian presented Ella to Morrigan. "For you, Ella, I wish the fae will forever be friends." Morrigan kissed Ella's forehead in turn.

Dorian presented Ella to Cassandra. "May you have the foresight to make wise decisions." Cassandra gave Ella a kiss.

Dorian knelt down so Sol could reach the baby. "I want baby Ella to always be happy. I want her to laugh a lot." Sol pressed a kiss to Ella's cheek.

Then, Dorian brought Ella to Eeva. "I hope that you will

easily find love and kindness, Ella." Eeva sealed her blessing with a kiss.

Dorian approached Sawyer, and Sawyer gazed down at the beautiful baby girl in his arms. Her wide, blue eyes looked directly at him as if she knew exactly what was happening. He smiled at the child. "Ella, I wish that you will always see the wonder of the natural world around you." He leaned down and brushed his lips against the baby's soft, fine hair.

Dorian moved on, presenting Ella to Tara. "May you have balance, baby Ella, to never feel overwhelmed by what you encounter along the way." Tara kissed the child's head.

Dorian next presented her to Hazel. "May you be a force to reckon with." And Hazel kissed the baby.

Dorian then stood before Piper. "I hope that you can always find solace in the stars, Ella." Piper placed a kiss on Ella's head.

Finally, Dorian presented Ella to Devan. "May you learn from your mistakes." Devan leaned down and kissed the child.

Taking his place beside his husband again, Dorian passed Ella to him. Then, he went to the altar and took a moon cookie from the plate and the chalice of faux mead.

He held up the cookie. "May I never hunger," he said before eating it. "Blessed be." Then, he held the chalice aloft. "May I never thirst." He drank from it. "Blessed be."

Dorian took up the plate and chalice and turned to Ria. She followed his pattern, asking that she may never hunger or thirst. And so the ritual of cakes and ale continued around the circle, gently grounding the energies that had been raised.

After Dorian had offered the sustenance to Cory, he placed the plate and chalice onto the altar, took Ella back from Cory, and faced the circle.

"Thank you for your blessings. We will now release the circle," Cory told them. He turned to the altar. "God, Divine Father, Sacred Brother, we thank you for joining us. Go if you must. Stay if you will." Cory snuffed out the god's candle.

"Goddess, Divine Mother, Sacred Sister, thank you for joining us. Go if you must. Stay if you will." Then he snuffed out the goddess's candle.

They all turned North, and Cory continued. "Spirits of the North, element of Earth, thank you for joining us. Go if you must. Stay if you will."

They turned West. "Spirits of the West, element of Water, thank you for joining us. Go if you must. Stay if you will."

Again, they turned South. "Spirits of the South, element of Fire, thank you for joining us. Go if you must. Stay if you will." And Cory snuffed out the Fire candle.

Finally, they turned East. "Spirits of the East, element of Air, thank you for joining us. Go if you must. Stay if you will."

As everyone turned back into the circle, Cory said, "The circle is open but never broken. Blessed be."

"Blessed be!" everyone answered.

CHAPTER 33

Evergreen sat cross-legged beside Sawyer on the floor of the common room as Dorian and Cory opened the gifts everyone had gotten for baby Ella. Evergreen had given her a dream catcher for her bedroom.

Everyone's attention was on the couple as they smiled and expressed their thanks. Baby Ella wasn't much interested in her presents, but she watched curiously from her car seat.

Muir and Larkspur played with a discarded ribbon bow nearby, sometimes batting at it, sometimes picking it up and playing keep away.

Evergreen's legs started to tingle painfully from sitting in the same position for too long. She stretched them out, crossing them at the ankles, and leaned back. But as she placed her hand on the floor behind her, her fingers landed on Sawyer's.

Her heart jumped, and she glanced over at him. His wide eyes softened, and he smiled gently at her.

"Oops, sorry," she murmured, shifting her weight and moving her hand from his.

"It's okay," he answered with a nod.

She directed her gaze back to Dorian and Cory, who were holding up a handmade crib mobile with sacred symbols dangling from it. A moment later, Evergreen's breath hitched as Sawyer's hand covered hers. The slight pressure, the warmth, a jolt ran through her, and her nerves stood on end.

She looked over at Sawyer again. His eyes were soft and solicitous. "Is this okay?" he whispered.

Evergreen nodded once, not sure her voice would be stable enough to answer. Her consent was rewarded when Sawyer gave her a brilliant smile. Her breath left her in a rush as if she'd been kicked in the chest. That look, that light in his eyes. Only in her most outlandish dreams had Sawyer ever looked at her like that. It was the gaze that said all his little kindnesses had meant something. It said he'd never forgotten her.

Warmth bloomed in her chest. A pleasant ache squeezed her heart, an ache of anticipation, an ache that made promises.

Evergreen averted her gaze, not wanting to draw attention only slightly more than wanting to keep her eyes locked with his. She couldn't have said how long they sat like that, but it was long enough for her hand to miss the feel of his when he pulled away.

All in all, the naming ceremony had been a resounding success. They all welcomed Ella to the path and wished that her journey would be more full of love, laughter, and learning than theirs had been thus far.

As Evergreen lay beside Sawyer in the dark meditation room that evening, she stared up at the starry night sky, stroking Muir beside her. The room was silent but for the whir of the space heater, and that silence was thick and oppressive.

"Do you remember when we all went on that trip to the beach?" Evergreen asked, the words squeezed out of her as if from the pressure of the silence.

"Yeah, that was the summer before my senior year. Wasn't it? We went for the solstice. Piper was so disappointed that we couldn't see as many stars as she'd thought we would be able to," he answered. "She moped the whole time."

"But Hazel was happy," Evergreen countered.

"Oh, I don't think I've seen Hazel happier. But then again, she's a sea witch, so that's to be expected."

Evergreen giggled under her breath. "That's true. I think that was our first trip with Cory, too. Wasn't it?" She glanced over at Sawyer, who nodded, still staring up at the ceiling.

"Yeah, Dorian and Cory had just gotten together. Remember they kept sneaking off to be alone thinking no one would notice?"

"Oh my gods, and Devan kept getting lost," she added, laughing louder.

Sawyer chuckled, and the sound made Evergreen shiver like a string that had been plucked. "Do you think that the reason he's always late is because he has a horrible sense of direction?" he asked, glancing over at her.

Their eyes locked, and Evergreen's smile relaxed. "I bet you're right," she murmured, her response coming out quiet and confused as if she'd forgotten his question.

The silence squeezed her lungs, and her breaths were slow but shallow.

Sawyer's eyes were steady and earnest, and she knew what

he wanted. She was certain her expression wasn't much different. He propped himself up on his elbow, staring down at her with intent.

Evergreen's heart raced, and the sweet ache of desire spread through her core. As he leaned down closer, she closed her eyes, anticipation making her body hum.

When he kissed her, it wasn't as sweet and fleeting as the first time. His lips were insistent, fiery and fierce as they branded hers. She lifted her head to match his urgency.

And then, a loud trilling sounded in her ear as Muir complained that she'd stopped petting him.

Sawyer pulled away. He turned to the cat and laughed. The sound of his chuckle broke the moment far more than Muir's interruption.

Then, Sawyer reached out and scratched Muir's ears. "Well, all right then," he told him.

The cat flopped down on his side and rolled onto his back.

"Is this a trap?" Sawyer asked him.

"No, Muir actually likes belly rubs. He must like you if he's offering you his belly," Evergreen said.

Sawyer stroked Muir's chest and stomach, and the cat wiggled, unable to sit still in his excitement. "You're a funny one," Sawyer told him.

Evergreen smiled at the pair. "You're in trouble now. He's not going to leave you alone after this."

"That's fine," Sawyer answered, glancing back up at her. His smile was soft and warm, the passionate heat mellowed in his eyes. "We should probably try to go to sleep," he said. "I'm sure your mom has something planned for us all tomorrow. We wouldn't want to miss it."

Evergreen nodded, her disappointment tempered with the thought that she finally knew what old movie kisses felt like.

CHAPTER 34

Sawyer didn't think he'd ever felt as good as he did the next morning. The sun shined brightly off the snow, and the outside world sparkled as if covered in eco-friendly glitter. His chest was warm, his heart light, and his head fuzzy as if he lay on a bed of pink cotton candy.

Eeva and Muir no longer lay beside him, but that didn't dampen his mood. Anticipation zipped through him, and he knew he wore a goofy, self-satisfied smile as he changed his clothes.

The pressure of his joy built up inside him, and he felt as if he'd have to shout at the top of his lungs just to let off some of the steam.

He took a deep breath, pushed his shoulders back, and strode into the common room. Eeva sat on the couch, Muir pawing at her as he placed himself between her and the book she was trying to read.

"Yes, yes, I see you, Muir," she murmured, bookmarking her page and redirecting her attention to her furbaby.

"Good morning," Sawyer greeted, confident she couldn't see his silly grin from this distance.

But as she looked over in his direction and visibly held in a giggle, he was certain she'd still heard it. "Morning," she returned.

He got control of his expression as he crossed the room and sat on the couch beside her, his gaze landing on the cup of coffee on the table next to her cocoa. "Is someone else sitting here?" he asked, pointing at the cup.

"No," she said. "That's for you."

"Thank you." His smile returned without consent. "Any idea what the plans are for today?"

Eeva shook her head.

Even her shaking her head is cute, Sawyer thought.

"Hmm. Well, we still haven't made the soap and shampoo for the gift baskets. We haven't made the candles for Yule yet either. And we don't have a Yule log. Dad will probably wait a few days before he really starts cooking. So my guess is one of those three things."

It turned out Eeva's guess was correct. Once everyone had breakfasted, Ria said they would be making soap and shampoo that day. Because they didn't have the knowledge to deal with the volatile chemicals involved in from scratch soap making, Eeva and Sawyer were put in charge of the essential oils that would be used as fragrance.

They sat at the dining room table while they let some of the others do the hard work in the kitchen.

"What do you think of ylang ylang?" Sawyer asked, reading the bottle he'd just smelled.

Eeva shrugged. "It's all right. I like jasmine better. Oh, how about this one." She held out the vial to him, and he leaned forward to sniff it.

"That one is nice," he said.

"It's nag champa. Yeah, I like it, too."

"Should we try mixing some together?" he asked.

"Yeah, I got my mom's chart with base, middle, and top notes." She drew the paper toward her, squinting at it as she read. Then she offered it to him so he could make his own blends.

They focused on their tasks for a bit, Eeva muttering to herself in concentration. Her eyebrows were pulled together as she carefully counted out the drops of oil from the eyedropper.

As she took a test sniff, she smiled, sighing in contentment at her creation. When she looked up at him, he realized he hadn't been focusing on his own work at all.

"Do you want to smell? I think it turned out pretty good," she said, holding it out to him.

"Sure." He leaned forward just as she moved to bring the vial closer to his nose. The glass bumped his nose, and he snuffled as the scent overpowered him.

Eeva burst into laughter. "Oh gods, sorry," she managed through her giggles. "Are you okay?"

The sound of her mirth tightened his chest in the most pleasant way. "I'm fine," he said, unable to hold back a smile in the face of her glee.

"I'll go get you some coffee beans. Maybe that will clear the scent out of your nose."

She got up from the table and went to the kitchen, returning a few moments later with a glass jar of coffee beans. "Here," she said, offering him the jar.

He opened it and breathed deep. The earthy scent overtook the smell of her blend.

Before he put the cap back on, Eeva leaned over him and stuck her nose in the jar. She breathed deep then sighed. "I always loved the smell of coffee," she said. "I wish it tasted as good as it smells."

"It does. Your palate is just too unrefined to appreciate it," Sawyer teased.

Eeva made a choking sound then laughed as she straightened up. "Whatever. Your palate is just so dead that you need something that strong to taste at all. That's why you like spicy food, too."

"You're just a wimp when it comes to real flavor. That's why you can't handle spicy food."

She laughed again. "It's true. I am a wimp when it comes to spicy food. But, seriously, what is everyone's deal with liking spicy food? I mean, there are other flavors: sweet, salty, savory. Why does *everyone* want spicy?"

Sawyer just smiled at her impassioned speech, reveling in the comfortable atmosphere they had found.

"Oh my gods, this one time, my friend from college—he's the president of the Indian Student Association. He invited me to their Diwali celebration. Anyway, they had tons of Indian food there, right? And I could smell that it was spicy before I even put it in my mouth. But I really wanted to try it, so I asked him which stuff wasn't spicy. He said none of them were. So I trusted him, you know? Lies, so many lies. Do you know how much naan I had to eat to cool my mouth down? Man, it's like a slow burn, too. You take the first bite, and you're like, 'this is good.' Then four or five bites in, it just hits you. And it stays long after you've finished. Have you ever tried Indian food?"

Sawyer couldn't keep the grin from his face as Eeva told her story. It reminded him of before, when she was talkative and open. He was glad she hadn't lost that part of herself. "I have," he answered. "It's really good. Curry is great on winter days like this. It will warm you right up."

Eeva pursed her lips in disappointment. "I wish I could eat curry. It always looks so good."

"I could make you some," Sawyer offered. "If I blend my own curry powder, I can take out all the spicy elements."

"You can cook?" she asked, tilting her head.

Sawyer snorted. "I am a grown man, you know."

"I see that," she said, her tone carrying the tint of appreciation.

CHAPTER 35

Evergreen's anxiety had started to wane as she went about making tea the next morning. Sawyer had been sweet and playful all the day prior. The atmosphere around them had been easy, much easier than in the past. There was no better feeling than the person you like liking you back.

And though the world seemed to shine around her, the anxiety didn't go away completely. There was something fragile in this stage. His actions said he was attracted to her more than he liked her, and he hadn't said anything one way or the other. She still didn't really know about his life at the moment. And the fact that they would be leaving in less than a week hung over her, a looming presence that she couldn't quite ignore no matter how good she felt.

Still, she tried her best to ignore it, having faith that they would at least talk about what would happen later before they left.

At breakfast, her mother worried that there was still too

much to do before Yule. "We still don't have a Yule log," she said. "I completely forgot to harvest one at Midsummer. And now we don't have time for a fresh one to dry out before the solstice."

"Don't worry, Mom," Evergreen comforted. "I'm sure there's a downed tree in the woods. We can just go out there and saw off a log. It's better that way anyway. And then it'll only have to dry for a few days just to get the surface moisture out."

"I'd go soon if I were you," Cory said. "There's a storm coming."

"The news said we would get a dusting tomorrow," Wes agreed.

"No," Cory shook his head. "It'll be worse than that."

Ria made an anxious sound.

"It's all right, Ria," Sawyer soothed. "Eeva and I can go out today and find one. We were tramping around the woods a few days ago, and I saw a few downed trees that might do."

"Would you?" Ria asked.

Sawyer looked to Evergreen for support. "Yeah, sure thing, Mom. I'll go get the handsaw from the garage, and we can start looking right away."

Evergreen heard her father say he would pack them a lunch again as she went to the garage. When she returned, Sawyer was putting on his winter things. She put down the saw and did the same.

"Make sure you bundle up," Ria said. "The temperature is dropping."

They did as they were told. Sawyer picked up the saw, and Evergreen carried the lunch her father had made for them.

Then, they waved goodbye and told everyone they'd be back before dark.

Evergreen followed Sawyer through the woods, trailing him to the downed trees he'd remembered. The first two hadn't been dead long enough for the wood to season properly.

"There's one more," he said, leading the way.

Luckily, that tree had sat long enough that it would burn nicely after a few days of drying out.

"Could you hold that end?" Sawyer asked.

Evergreen got down on her knees, the snow seeping into her jeans, to hold the log steady so he could saw it.

It took a while for him to saw through it, much longer than she would have expected. By the time he was finished, it was well past lunch time.

"The temperature really has dropped," he commented. "Why don't we head to the isolation cabin and have lunch? We aren't far now. We could make a fire and warm up before heading back."

"Sounds good," Evergreen agreed, trying to stop her teeth from chattering.

"Be careful," Sawyer advised as he went ahead of her on the path, the log in his arms. "There's a slope coming up, and it's probably icy with the temperature change. Ohhhh—"

Sawyer slid down the hill, crashing at the bottom.

"Sawyer, are you okay?" Evergreen shouted, her voice raising in pitch in her alarm. She sat on her butt and slid down the icy hill.

"I'm fine," he muttered. "Only my pride is hurt."

Evergreen offered her hand and hauled him up.

He hissed in pain.

"What is it? Are you hurt?"

"It's okay. I think I just twisted my ankle. It just smarts a little. I'm fine."

Evergreen gnawed her lips, her stomach churning. "Let's get you inside. Just leave the log there. I'll come back for it. Lean on me."

He wrapped his arm around her shoulders and leaned some of his weight on her as they walked. After she'd gotten him settled on a blanket on the floor of the isolation cabin, she returned for the log, the saw, and the lunch bag. She placed the log and the saw in a corner of the cabin, put the lunch bag on the table, then went out to the wood hutch to get dry firewood.

"Will you call my mom and tell her we're going to wait a bit before coming back while I make a fire?"

"I'll be fine," Sawyer argued. "I can walk as soon as I have lunch and warm up. Look, it's not even swollen. I just twanged it."

Evergreen frowned. "Well, let's see how you feel after you eat."

As the fire crackled in the hearth, Evergreen unpacked their lunch and set it on the coffee table as before. She watched Sawyer while he ate.

"You worrying like that isn't going to make it better faster," he pointed out.

Evergreen sighed. "I know. I'm sorry. I just hate it when people get hurt."

Sawyer smiled. "I know. You sort of feel it, too. Don't you? You get all queasy in your gut, like you're going to be sick."

"How did you know? Does that happen to you, too?"

Sawyer shook his head. "No, but you aren't the only empath

I know. My friend Flick is like that. She can't even take her dog to the vet without feeling sick."

Evergreen remembered the name from his social media, back when she'd still checked his profile every day. "She's a friend from school?" she asked, not sure she really wanted to know but unable to stop herself.

"Yeah." He didn't elaborate.

Evergreen's stomach hardened in a flash of jealousy. She shook her head to rid herself of the feeling.

After they'd finished their lunch, Evergreen told him to take off his shoes so she could see his ankle. The fire had sufficiently warmed the room enough that she took off her coat and boots as well. She sat on her feet, patting her thighs to tell him to put his foot there. He did.

Evergreen felt around his ankle carefully, her fingertips prodding for any puffiness. She didn't find any.

"Okay, now rotate your ankle for me," she directed. "Does it hurt at all?"

Sawyer shook his head. "Nope. I'm okay, Doc. No pain at all. Am I good to go?"

Evergreen chuckled, her worry filtering out with each laugh. "I think you'll live."

A chiming melody emanated from Evergreen's pocket. She dug into it and answered her mother's call. "Hey, what's up, Mom?"

"Evergreen Pendre, where in goddess's green earth are you?" she shouted.

"We're at the isolation cabin. We just had lunch. Sawyer fell, so I wanted to make sure he wasn't hurt before we headed back. But he's fine, so we're just about to leave."

"Oh thank goodness," Ria said with a sigh. "Listen, you guys just stay there. Okay? Don't try to come back until the storm blows over. There should be snacks enough in the cupboards, and there are blankets in the trunk."

"What storm?" Evergreen said, going to the window. She couldn't even see the trees through the blowing snow. "Oh," she answered flatly. "Yeah, okay. We'll stay put. But can you feed Muir? He gets a half can of wet food at seven."

"I'll take care of him," her mother confirmed before hanging up.

Evergreen returned to Sawyer on the floor. "I guess we're stuck here for a while," she said, putting her phone on the table beside his.

"Guess so," he murmured, shifting his gaze to the fire.

As the logs cracked in the hearth and the wind began to howl, Evergreen's awareness fixed on Sawyer. He seemed relaxed, his legs stretched out in front of him. The glow from the fire played in his golden hair.

Without really thinking about it, Evergreen reached out and stroked a shiny lock. Sawyer's amber eyes met hers.

"Eeva," he murmured, his expression serious, "I don't know if this is the best time to tell you this, but—"

Evergreen silenced his words by covering his mouth with hers. Whatever he'd been trying to say must not have been very important because he met her demanding kiss with one of his own.

A shiver ran through her as he slipped his hand into her hair, pulling her closer with urgency. She gasped against his mouth when his hot tongue flicked her lower lip.

He pulled back, his brow furrowed despite the desire in his eyes. "Was that okay?" he asked, his voice breathy and deep.

Evergreen sat up and climbed on top of him, smiling as his hard manhood dug against her through their jeans. She wrapped her arms around his neck, playing with the hair at the base of his head. "Perfect," she responded.

Sawyer didn't need any more encouragement. He kissed her again, roughly grabbing her ass as she straddled him.

She moaned against his mouth, the sensation tickling her lips.

Sawyer slipped his hands under the back of her shirt, his rough fingertips sending a thrill up her spine as he stroked her bare flesh. "You're so beautiful, Eeva," he murmured, pressing insistent kisses to her throat.

Lust raged inside her, urgent, demanding. She arched her back, grinding hard against him. "Do you have a condom?" she whispered, her voice thick and raw even to her own ears.

He flinched beneath her. She pulled back, staring at him. "No," he said with a grimace.

"It's okay. There's still hope." She climbed off him and made her way over to the blanket chest. Digging through the blankets, her hand touched the smooth plastic wrapper. She turned back around, holding up a strip of condoms in triumph.

"Why would that be here?" Sawyer asked.

"Does it matter?"

"No, I'm just curious."

"My parents keep the cabin stocked with condoms in case someone is too sexually pent up to properly meditate." Evergreen shrugged. "Easier clean up. You aren't allergic to latex are you?"

"No, you?"

Evergreen grinned. "Nope. Isn't that lucky?"

"I certainly feel like it's my lucky day. Do you mind coming over here please?"

"Oh, I do hope so," Evergreen said with a chuckle, swaying her hips as she returned to Sawyer.

He laughed at her double entendre. "Don't worry about that," he promised.

"Oooo, look who's so confident now." Evergreen smoothly climbed back on top of him and wrapped her legs around him.

"Oh, I've a right to be. Here, let me show you." He removed his shirt, his golden hair getting deliciously tousled.

"You do that then," Evergreen encouraged, placing her palm on his firm chest before kissing him.

Evergreen shivered as he removed her shirt, the cabin not nearly as warm as she'd thought. "Do you need help with my bra?" she asked.

He snorted then smirked before unclasping it with one hand.

I guess not, she thought, grinning.

His skin burned hers as he pressed her to him, smothering her thoughts with sensations. She gasped for air, her desire even more urgent than it had been before she'd gotten the condoms.

He shifted under her, picking her up and laying her on her back atop the clothes they'd discarded.

He stroked his fingers down her body, his touch feather-light and maddening. Her clit throbbed as he unbuttoned her jeans. His eyes were fixed on hers as he slowly unzipped them. "Tell me when you're ready," he requested.

"I'm already there," she informed, not at all surprised that it hadn't taken more foreplay. *It is Sawyer after all,* she reasoned. *And I've been waiting a long time for this.*

He obligingly removed her pants and underwear, the fabric rubbing roughly against her smooth skin. He smirked, the expression confident and irritating somehow as he unbuttoned his own jeans.

"You tease," Evergreen accused.

He chuckled but didn't argue. The rest of his discarded clothes made a satisfying fwump as he dropped them on the floor.

Evergreen's breaths came out heavy and slow as she watched Sawyer roll the condom onto his ready cock. She grinned at the glistening drop of precum at the tip. She sat up and wrapped her fingers around the solid shaft.

Sawyer shuddered under her hand, his breath coming out in a rush.

"Feel good?" she asked.

He nodded, his eyes losing focus as she stroked. "I'm not selfish," he muttered, his weak voice pleasing her just as much as his shivers.

Evergreen bit her lip against her moan, her body shaking as he ran the pad of his thumb over her clit. Her hand on his cock loosened.

Sawyer kissed her, slowly lowering her back to the floor. Her thighs twitched in anticipation as his cock neared her core. And as he slid smoothly into her, the howling wind outside did not cover the sounds of their mutual pleasure.

Sawyer pumped slow and hard, his hips digging into Evergreen's thighs. She vaguely wondered if she'd have bruises the next day. But she didn't care. It was finally happening. With Sawyer. His abs stiffened with each thrust, and Evergreen clung to his neck and shoulders, her fingernails sinking into his skin. And as he drove her to her peak, she knew that he'd had the right to brag after all.

He collapsed beside her, having fully lived up to expectations and then some. His eyelids drooped.

Evergreen stroked his sweaty hair. "Tired?" she murmured.

He nodded.

She glanced over at the window. "It's dark out. Go to sleep," she encouraged, leaning over to kiss his cheek.

He nodded again but held his arms out to her.

She smiled and snuggled in close to him, his heartbeat a comforting lullaby.

Sometime in the night, Evergreen awoke. She wiggled free from Sawyer's embrace and started toward the bathroom.

The fire had dimmed, so she stopped and put a few more logs in. Standing up again, she looked back to make sure she hadn't woken him. Her phone's notification light blinked from the table, and she picked it up to make sure her mother wasn't freaking out.

By the time she'd realized it was Sawyer's phone, it was too late. She'd already seen part of the message from a woman named Maria, whose profile picture was a black cat. "Hey, honey, call or text me when you get this…" The rest of the message was cut off, and she didn't know the password to see what else was said even if she'd wanted to.

Evergreen's stomach dropped, and she was pretty certain she was going to be sick. She put the phone back on the table and rushed to the bathroom. After turning on the cold water, she splashed her face. She took deep breaths, trying to keep her lunch down.

Who the fuck is Maria? she thought. *Does Sawyer have a girlfriend? Is that what he was trying to tell me when I cut him off by kissing him? Would he cheat on his girlfriend with me? I never thought he was that kind of guy. Maybe he isn't. Maybe he's poly. Maybe that's what he was trying to tell me. I mean, that's great for him or whatever. But poly doesn't work for me. I don't share.*

Once the initial nausea had quieted, Evergreen's chest tightened as if some witch hunter was trying to force her to confess. *I knew it*, she thought. *I should have listened to my instincts from the beginning.*

Hot tears rolled down her cheeks, and her nose burned as she tried to silence the sob that rose in her throat.

CHAPTER 36

Before Sawyer even opened his eyes the next morning, he smiled to himself. He was groggy, sore, in that very satisfying way. Eeva no longer lay on his chest, but the scratchy roughness of the blanket she'd draped over his naked body bespoke her care. He'd gotten through to her. She might have cut off his confession by kissing him, but he'd made sure that his actions spoke louder than words ever could. He breathed deep from his nose and cracked his eyelids against the morning light.

Eeva lay, fully dressed, on a separate blanket. She stared up at the ceiling, her eyes dark and puffy.

Sawyer rolled to his side, facing her. "Good morning," he greeted warmly. "Did you sleep okay?"

She didn't turn to him. She just stared ahead, her eyes unfocused and resolute. "That was a mistake," she declared, her tone deadpan.

It took Sawyer's mind a few seconds to process her words.

As his heart squeezed, his stomach churned. "You regret it?" he asked, not even certain he'd said it loud enough for her to hear.

"Yes," she confirmed. "I regret it."

The room spun as Sawyer seemed to drown in a sudden sense of hopelessness. *Did something happen?* He wondered, his mind grasping for some explanation. *She certainly seemed to enjoy it last night. Did I misunderstand? But she initiated it to begin with.*

He tried to swallow around the lump in his throat. *But that doesn't really matter. Does it? She has the right to feel differently in the light of day. But...did I do something wrong?*

Sawyer analyzed her stony expression. She wasn't giving anything away. "Okay," he muttered. *What else can I even say?* he thought. *If that's how she feels, then that's how she feels.*

He averted his eyes, praying that he could hold it together. Sitting up, he held the blanket to his naked form. He grabbed his clothes, his numb fingers hardly registering the feel of the fabric in his hand. Then he went to the bathroom to dress. His movements were slow and automatic, relying on muscle memory to execute the procedure.

He glanced at himself in the mirror as he moved to put his shirt on. There were tiny indentations on his shoulders and back where Eeva had dug her nails into him. He pulled on his shirt, covering the evidence. But as the cloth passed over his face, he was smacked with Eeva's scent. *That's right,* he thought. *She lay on my clothes as we made love...had sex,* he corrected.

He turned on the faucet and closed his eyes against the telltale burning. He breathed in deep through his tingling nose, but he didn't manage to keep all the tears down. He bent over the sink and splashed water on his face, washing away the few that had escaped.

By the time he exited the bathroom, he had successfully masked his emotions. He walked over to the window and looked out. "The snow has stopped. We should head back," he said, woodenly.

When Eeva didn't respond, he glanced over at her. *Bad idea,* he thought, redirecting his eyes as his stomach flopped.

"I'll carry the log if you can get the saw and lunch bag," Sawyer said, not daring to look at her again. His voice sounded hollow even to him, and he knew he'd never talked to Eeva that way before.

She didn't respond, but she didn't argue either. Sawyer pulled on his winter things and picked up the log. Her footsteps were soft as she drifted after him.

With how bad the storm had looked the night before, Sawyer had expected the snow would be a lot deeper. Still, it was about mid-shin for him, and it took a bit of effort to stomp through it. He was extra careful when he climbed the hill he'd fallen down the day before. And he did warn Eeva to watch out, as if he were a guide she'd paid to get her home safely.

As they arrived back at the retreat center, they were greeted with exclamations of joy and relief. The enthusiasm from his friends and family was too loud, too happy, too juxtaposed to the weight that silently crushed him.

"I'm just tired," he found himself saying as someone asked him what was wrong. He wasn't even sure who it had been. Probably his mom. There didn't seem to be a lot of attention on him, so he didn't bother to figure it out.

He registered a gentle pat on the back. "Maybe a nice hot

shower will sort you out." Yes, it was his mom speaking. He nodded, passed the Yule log into Wes's arms, and headed in the direction of the bathroom. He turned on the shower, the mundane task doing little to distract his thoughts.

He needed a shower to be sure. He could feel the dried sweat, no longer sticky, still clinging to him like Eeva had just hours before. The ghostly remnants of her kisses on his mouth, his face, his neck and chest, still echoed in his mind. He needed a shower, but he didn't want one. He didn't want to wash her off of him, as if doing so would wipe their too short time together away like it never happened.

No, he thought. *It had happened.* The ache in his chest was too real, and it wasn't going away just by washing the only evidence of their love…sex down the drain. He'd wished it was only that easy, that fifteen minutes of soap and hot water could rewind time, back to when he still had hope in his heart.

He stepped under the waterfall showerhead, the sound of the water splashing on the stone walls and floor too pleasantly dissonant, and went about erasing all physical traces of their night together, the night she regretted so much. How much of what streaked down Sawyer's face was tears? How much was water? He didn't give it much thought.

CHAPTER 37

A shower had not washed away all traces of Sawyer from Evergreen's thoughts. She'd said she regretted their night together, and she did. She regretted how she now had to deal with the emotional fallout. She had gone against her better judgment. Her heart had opened up to him again, called out to him again, seemingly forgetting the hurt it had gone through before. She'd been weak. Sawyer was her weakness. And now she would pay for it.

She would pay for it every time her eyes drifted toward him, every time her skin remembered the brush of his touch, and every time he didn't give her a second thought. Her legs were still sore from where his hip bones had pounded into her. And, despite her emotions, her body was still languid from the satisfaction he'd provided.

"Okay," she muttered to herself, repeating Sawyer's words to her declaration that morning.

She stood at the kitchen island, cutting cotton string into

two-foot lengths. Cassandra stood at the stove melting beeswax in the double boiler.

Okay? Evergreen thought. Is that all he could say? Didn't he want to know why I suddenly changed my mind? I thought there was going to be more of a fight. I thought I was going to get to tell him exactly why I was upset. But he just accepted it. Just like that. It must not have been that important to him to begin with. I mean, he shrugged it off so easily. Shrugged it off while I lay there despondent and hurting.

Evergreen had tried to feel out his reaction at the time. But when her own emotions were that high, she couldn't effectively read others.

I'm so stupid, she thought miserably. *I wish I never would have come home for Yule. If I would have stayed at school, Sawyer could have stayed a relatively happy memory. Sure, I would have been hurt that he'd left and never looked back. But at least I remembered him as sweet, and kind, and solid. Now...it just stings to think about him at all.*

"Okay," she said again, clicking her tongue in disgust.

"What are you muttering about over there?" Cassandra asked from the stove.

Evergreen flinched. "Nothing," she murmured. She started tying washers to the ends of the strings she'd cut.

"Mmmm, yeah, I'm not buying it. You've been weird since you got back this morning. Did something happen between you and Sawyer?"

Evergreen turned her back to her cousin, knowing she wouldn't be able to control her expression. "No," she said, trying for unconcerned. "Why would you think that?"

"Um, I don't know," Cassandra said sarcastically. "Maybe

because you two have been flirting with each other since you arrived, and now you can't even look at each other."

Evergreen didn't respond.

"Did you two have a fight?" Cassandra pushed.

Evergreen sighed. Hanging one of the strings over a wire coat hanger, she carried it to the stove.

Cassandra took it from her and started ladling melted wax over the string.

"I guess you could say he isn't who I thought he was," Evergreen murmured.

Cassandra responded without looking away from her work. "Did you think he wouldn't have changed at all over the last four and a half years?"

"No, I mean, I knew he would. Of course he would. But…it just seemed like he'd changed for the better up until yesterday."

"You want to be more specific about what exactly happened?"

"No."

"Okay…Well, from where I stand—knowing what little I know—Sawyer is a pretty good guy. I mean, I think we can both agree I have an eye for irresponsible assholes. Not to mention I'm a magnet for them."

Evergreen didn't say anything.

"We've all known each other for a long time. And let's not mince words here. You've been totally in love with him for most of that time."

Evergreen made a sound to protest, but a glance from her cousin just made her nod her head silently.

"That's a long time fantasizing and hoping and wishing."

Cassandra shrugged. "Maybe you've put him on a bit of a pedestal. Don't you think that's possible?"

Evergreen frowned. "Even if that's true—and I'm not saying it is—there are certain things that…just don't mesh between us."

"Such as…?"

"Well…I mean, yeah, we have known each other for a long time. But a lot of that time, he utterly pretended like he didn't know me at all. Like, he left for college and didn't talk to me at all until just a few days ago."

Cassandra snorted. "He ignored you, did he? So you sent him message after message, and he just pretended like he didn't know you? Be honest, cuz. Communication is a two-way street. Sure, maybe he didn't reach out to you, but I don't recall you reaching out to him either."

Evergreen shifted her weight uncomfortably from foot to foot. "I mean…that's true…but—"

"Look, I'm not trying to assign blame to either one of you. I'm just pointing out that you two have a pretty long history of not being honest with each other. You never told him how you felt back then. You didn't reach out when you missed him. And he's obviously got some things to answer for, too. So don't you think it's possible that whatever you're upset about is just a misunderstanding?"

Evergreen's stomach rolled as she remembered reading the text on Sawyer's phone. She shook her head. "I hear what you're saying. And, yeah, I haven't been very good at communicating with him. But this time…I don't see how I could be misunderstanding."

Cassandra shrugged. "Well, it's not like I even know the

particulars, so maybe you're right. But it's still four days until Yule. I suggest you figure something out."

"It's a big house. There are a lot of people. We can pretty well avoid each other for four days."

"If you say so."

CHAPTER 38

Sawyer had done a pretty good job of avoiding Eeva since they'd returned, though effectively doing so meant he was overly aware of her movements. Sometimes, he felt as if he could feel her eyes on him. But he told himself that was his imagination. That's what he wanted to believe. He wanted her to change her mind back, to return to the Eeva who would haunt him, the one who'd climbed into his lap with that come-hither smile.

He was exhausted, physically and emotionally. But he didn't want to go to sleep. He didn't want to crawl into his sleeping bag on the floor beside her. And he was worried what he would dream about. So he stayed up, sitting in the common room until everyone had gone to bed but him and his mom. Muir and Larkspur both lay in his lap as he stroked them in unison.

"Are you going to tell me what happened, son?" Tara asked finally.

"I don't want to talk about it," he murmured.

"Are you sure? Because you kind of have that expression like you need to."

Sawyer frowned, a tug of war playing out in his mind. "I think I fucked up."

"How's that?" his mom asked.

"Eeva…" He choked a little on her name. "We uh… Stuff happened last night while we were in the isolation cabin."

"Is that your way of telling me you and Eeva had sex?"

Sawyer nodded slightly.

"Okay. So how did you fuck up? You used protection, didn't you?"

"Yeah, we did…I…I wish I knew what I did wrong. I thought everything was great. Totally fine. Then I woke up this morning, and she's all serious… She said it was a mistake."

Tara nodded slowly, her eyes losing focus as she considered his problem. "Did she give you a reason?" she asked.

"No. And…it didn't feel right to ask. It's her body. If she regrets sharing it with me…then how can I argue?"

Tara reached out and rubbed her son's arm.

"Mom, what did I do? Why would she change her mind?"

Tara shook her head. "I don't know, honey. It could be any number of things. Maybe she got caught up in the moment and didn't really think about what it meant until after. Maybe, after all was done, she realized she felt more platonically toward you. Or maybe she's scared."

Though she had given her examples gently, each one was like a knife in Sawyer's chest. "Scared? Of me?" he asked.

Tara stroked her son's hair in the soothing gesture she'd always used when he was a boy. "Not necessarily," she answered. "She could be scared of what she felt, of what it could mean for her, for you, for your relationship."

"Like…like she's worried about getting hurt, so she pushed me away?"

"Well, that's one way of looking at it."

Sawyer frowned, gazing at the glowing embers in the hearth, all that was left of the fire that blazed only hours before. "But these explanations are really different. If she's scared, then I should reassure her. But if it's another reason, I should just leave her alone."

His mother nodded. "It is a predicament."

Could she just be scared? he wondered. He pictured the mask-like expression Eeva had worn as she'd said those three words: I regret it. *No,* he thought. *She wasn't scared. She never shied away from a confrontation. If she had something she wanted to say, she would have just said it.*

"I don't think she's scared, Mom," he admitted.

Tara sighed sadly. "I know it hurts right now. But it will get better. Believe me."

Sawyer dipped his head in a slow nod. He'd seen people go through much worse than what he was feeling, his mom included. But she was right. It didn't feel possible at the moment.

"You going to bed soon?" she asked.

"Yeah, in a bit. I'm just going to sit out here with the cats for a little while longer."

"Okay." She leaned over and pressed a kiss to her son's head. "Goodnight."

"Night, Mom."

As he turned his attention back to the glowing embers, his

phone vibrated in his pocket. The cats jumped up, looking at him with disdain at being disturbed. The deal was off. They went about their own cat business.

He opened a text from Felicity. It read, "Hey, bud. I've been thinking about you all day, and I'm getting a really weird vibe. Everything okay?"

Sawyer frowned. *Even states away I set off her empath alarm,* he thought. He texted her back. "Things are…pretty complicated over here. My mom and I are spending Yule with the old coven."

As he pressed the home button, Sawyer saw that he'd missed a text from Maria. "Hey, honey, call or text me when you get this. I know you said you were heading north for the holiday. I just saw on the news that a big storm is hitting up there. Just wanting to know you're all right."

It's too late to call her now, Sawyer thought. *I hope she hasn't been too worried.* He sent Maria a reply. "No worries. All good here. Hope all is well on your end, too. See you next week."

His phone buzzed with another message from Felicity. "Oh. Eeva must be there then. Do you want to talk about it?"

Sawyer's chest twinged. *I don't have the energy to talk about this anymore right now,* he thought. *Even with Flick.*

He replied with a simple, "later," and put his phone on the coffee table. With a sense of inevitability, he leaned to the side and let gravity flop him onto the couch. As he stared at the lights twinkling on the Yule tree, his eyes grew heavy, and he drifted off to sleep.

CHAPTER 39

Early the next morning, Evergreen was surprised to find that Sawyer was not in his sleeping bag. *He can't even stand to be near me now,* she thought. The action only confirmed his lack of concern in her mind.

After she made the daily offering of incense and lit the goddess candle at the altar, she went out into the sitting room. Sawyer lay on the couch, Muir curled up on his chest. *Traitor,* Evergreen thought, squinting at the cat. Though as soon as Muir saw her, he knew there was food in his bowl. He leapt off Sawyer and ran for the meditation room, the motion waking Sawyer from his sleep.

He looked around the room, confused, and froze as his gaze landed on Evergreen.

Her heart rate spiked, and there was an uncomfortably thick moment before she had the wherewithal to walk on through to the kitchen to make herself some tea. After sprinkling some cinnamon and sugar on her toast, the mundane task evening out her heartbeat, she moved to the dining room table to give him space to make coffee should he want it.

The atmosphere eased a bit the more people woke and joined her at the table.

"The next few days are going to be busy," Wes said as they all ate breakfast. "I'm making cookies today to put in the baskets so we can take them to the women's shelter tomorrow. And while we're in town tomorrow, I need to get some odds and ends so I can start cooking the day after."

"What kind of cookies are you making for the baskets?" Hazel asked.

"My grandmother's chocolate chip with vanilla buttercream frosting."

Everyone made yummy sounds.

"I'm going to need help decorating them if anyone is interested."

"Oh, me! Me!" Sol volunteered.

Wes smiled and nodded. "Eeva, how about you?"

"What?" Eeva said, her name pulling her out of her fuzzy-mindedness.

"Would you like to help Sol and me decorate cookies for the women's shelter?"

"Sure, Dad."

Cassandra also said she would help.

As Morrigan and Piper were talking about making the cards to put Sol's coloring masterpieces in, Sawyer burst out laughing. Everyone turned to him. He looked up from his phone.

"Speaking of holiday cards," he said. "Maria just sent me an ecard. Check this out."

Shame and irritation flooded into Evergreen. Even hearing her name on Sawyer lips, the lips that had so recently been pressed to her naked flesh, made her stomach drop.

Sawyer passed the phone to Tara, who giggled as she looked at it. Tara gave it to Devan, and so on until it reached Evergreen. She didn't want to look, but as Hazel handed it to her, she couldn't quell the compulsion.

On the screen was a picture of a woman and her cat. They wore matching elf hats with bells on the ends. They even had matching cuffs on their wrists. As Evergreen stared at the elderly woman grinning out at her, all the blood drained from her face. The room spun, and her toast felt like it was going to make a reappearance any second.

Eeva passed the phone to her dad, who laughed like everyone else.

"Who is this?" her mom asked when the phone had reached her.

"Maria." Sawyer answered. "She's the admin where I work. She's sort of like the mom of the whole place. Always looking out for everyone. She loves to dress her cat up, and we all get a big kick out of it."

Evergreen didn't say anything, couldn't have if she'd wanted to. She rose from her chair and left the dining room as quickly as she could without downright running. She could feel her heartbeat in her neck, her head, her fingertips as she made her way to the meditation room.

"Oh gods," she whispered, her voice strangled. "What have I done?"

Tears clouded her already imperfect vision, and there was

no stopping them from spilling down her face. *Why didn't I just talk to him?* she thought. *Why did I assume?*

She sucked in air, trying to breathe around her silent sobs. *It was perfect. He was perfect. And I had to go and fuck it up. He doesn't even know why I snubbed him. No wonder he can't even look at me.*

She froze, her tears halting as a thought occurred to her. *But if he really cared that much, why did he let go so easily? Because you told him it was a mistake, idiot,* she argued with herself. *But maybe...maybe it didn't mean as much to him as it did to me.*

She shook her head. *I can't know that for sure,* she thought. *Maybe he's just internalizing it like I was. Maybe he doesn't care as much as I do, and maybe he does. But I can't assume he doesn't. And I can't let my fear that he doesn't stop me from telling him. Because... because if he does...this is truly my last chance. It may already be too late.*

Evergreen sighed, squeezing her eyes shut. "Cassandra was right," she murmured. "It was a misunderstanding. If I let this stand without doing anything, I'm an even bigger coward than I was before. And anyway, no matter how it turns out, I can't let him believe that I really thought it was a mistake. Even if he doesn't care for me. That still would have hurt him."

Wiping her running nose on her sleeve, her head pounding from the tears she had shed, Evergreen crossed to the altar at the far end of the room. She dug through the cabinets underneath and pulled out three short sticks of incense.

She lit the first one from the already flickering goddess candle. "Artemis, please give me strength." She shook out the flame so that it could burn at a smolder and stuck it into the bucket of sand. Then, she lit the second. "Athena, please give me courage." She shook out the flame and put it beside the others. She lit the third. "Aphrodite, please smile on us both."

After she'd put the last incense stick in its place, she closed her eyes and bowed her head. Then, Evergreen took a deep breath, squared her shoulders, and let it out.

CHAPTER 40

As Ria, Hazel, and Cassandra used one side of the dining room table to start putting all the gifts into the baskets for the women's and children's shelter, Sawyer and Tara used the other end to cut circles of green cloth for the Yule charms everyone would be making.

Another tingle ran up Sawyer's spine, and he knew Eeva's eyes were on him again as she stood at the kitchen island decorating cookies with Wes, Cassandra, and Sol. Sawyer's heart squeezed in his already tight chest, but he didn't look over his shoulder at her.

Why? he wondered. *It feels like she has been looking at me constantly since breakfast. What does she want from me? Doesn't she know how painful this all is?*

Sawyer sighed, hanging his head as he leaned heavily on his hands on the table.

His mother patted his shoulder gently. "You all right?" she asked, her voice low.

He nodded. "Fine," he reassured, lifting his head and going back to his task.

It went on like that for the rest of the day. Sawyer tried to stay occupied, helping anyone with anything he could. It didn't matter if it was taking out the trash or changing Ella's diaper. He just wanted to stay busy. And through it all, he could feel Eeva's gaze following him.

I've got to be imagining things, he thought as everyone sat in the common room that evening. *I'm being paranoid.*

As was expected, Eeva headed to bed early. While she was saying her goodnights, Sawyer felt it again: the tingle, the little irritating prod. He looked up at her purposely for the first time since they'd left the isolation cabin, just to be sure he wasn't crazy. Her blue eyes were staring directly at him, intense despite her inability to see across the room in detail. His stomach wrenched, and he averted his gaze.

What the hell was that? he wondered. *What does she want from me? Is she messing with me? I never thought Eeva was someone who would play games.*

The strain that her attention caused eased as she went to bed, and Sawyer could breathe slightly better, though not freely.

Sawyer had planned to sleep on the couch again as he had the night before. He hadn't slept great, but he had slept. Still, his dreams had been full of vague feelings of impending doom, his anxiety filtering into his unconscious mind.

After everyone else had called it a night, Sawyer lay on the couch. He looked at his phone as another text came through on the group message Maria had started with his coworkers. Tim had sent a picture of him helping his daughter put the star atop their Christmas tree.

On one hand, Sawyer was grateful to Maria. She had given him the only bit of joy he'd felt that day by sharing the photo with her cat. And as everyone else had shared pictures of what they were up to in preparation of the holiday, it reminded Sawyer that there was a whole world outside of this retreat center, a whole world outside what he was feeling at the moment. Next week, he would be back at home in his one-bedroom apartment. He'd be back to work, taking care of all the injured and sick animals, covering the Christmas shift for his Christian coworkers.

On the other hand, the joy his friends and colleagues were experiencing was far different from what he was feeling. In some ways it made him feel a lot lonelier than he had before. Their smiles were foreign to him as if he couldn't figure out how to make his face look that way. And if he tried, it would be some grotesque mockery of the gesture that people would wince just looking at. Yes, next week he would be home. Eeva would be even further away than she was now, and he would be worse off than he was before he'd come, worse even than those days, months, years where he watched her live her life free of him via pictures on social media.

He was the only one now who hadn't added a picture to the group message. Sawyer placed his phone face down on the coffee table.

He shifted his gaze to the only light in the room, his eyes staring unfocused at the sparkling lights of the Yule tree. It was almost a relief to be alone. He could wallow without worrying anyone. Then again, there wasn't any pushing down his emotions when there was no one to pretend for.

"Sawyer?"

Sawyer flinched as he heard Eeva's voice whisper his name. He closed his eyes, wincing at the pain in his heart. *I'm hallucinating now. Great,* he thought.

But as he sighed deeply and reopened his eyes, Eeva really was standing there in the doorway. *Well, that's good. At least I'm not hearing things,* he thought.

He just stared at her, too tired to fight, his vision dull and unfocused. "What is it?" he muttered, his cheek misshapen against the couch as he hadn't bothered to lift his head. *Is that my voice?* he wondered, unable to believe that lost and lifeless tone came from his lips.

Eeva bit her lower lip, shifting her weight from one foot to the other. "N-never mind," she murmured. Then she turned around and headed back down the hall toward the meditation room.

Sawyer sighed again, staring at the tree lights once more. "Whatever," he muttered into the couch.

CHAPTER 41

Evergreen shook her head at herself as she stared at the ceiling of the meditation room the following morning.

"I can't believe you chickened out," she scolded herself, her disgust apparent in her tone.

But she could still hear the echo of Sawyer's voice as he said, "What is it?" Hollow, defeated. She had done that to him. She'd crushed him like that.

She'd thought perhaps he wasn't so affected by what she had said to him that cold morning in the isolation cabin. But that was clearly not the case. She could feel his despair, deep and thorny through the hum of her own nerves as she'd called out to him.

And just when she could put a stop to his sorrow, she fucking chickened out. *What if he can't forgive me?* she had wondered. And her words had stuck in her throat. She barely choked out "never mind" before she had to retreat, chased by her own fear and shame.

"Your fear got the better of you yesterday," she told herself. "But not today. Today, you are going to apologize and explain."

She crawled out of her sleeping bag and got dressed. She knew she was always the first to get up. She was the only morning person in the house. "Now is my chance," she said, trying to pump herself up. She opened the door to the meditation room and made her way to the living room.

Sawyer sat on the couch, rocking baby Ella in his arms.

"Thanks so much for holding her while I got her bottle ready," Dorian said, entering the room.

"No problem." Sawyer handed the baby back to her daddy, who sat in a nearby chair to feed her.

"You're up early," Evergreen murmured when Dorian's gaze fell on her.

"Yeah, Miss Ella here let us know she was hungry before her usual feeding time," Dorian explained.

Ella sucked happily at her breakfast.

Don't worry about it, Evergreen thought, soothing the disappointment that swirled in her gut. *You have time. You have the whole day. You got this.*

The baskets for the shelter were finished. They were stuffed full of hats, mittens, soap, shampoo, washcloths, cookies, and hand-colored pictures from Sol. It was finally time to deliver them. Evergreen got into her mom's car along with Tara, Hazel, and Piper. Wes had taken Devan and Sawyer with him to the grocery.

As Ria parked on the side of the road in front of the shelter, Evergreen took her cane from her bag and made her way to the front door. She pushed the buzzer as everyone else went to the trunk for the baskets.

"Yes?" the box crackled at her.

"We have some donations," Evergreen explained to the woman on the other side.

The door unlocked with a loud bzzzt, and Evergreen held it open for everyone, their hands full. She followed them inside, stopping behind them at the reception desk. The receptionist pointed them down the hall to where they could deliver the donations.

Evergreen could already feel a shadow falling over her heart, the pain and fear palpable in the air. "I think I'll just wait here," she told her mom. She reached her hand into her coat pocket and cursed when she realized she hadn't brought her hematite with her.

"We won't be long," Ria promised.

Evergreen turned to sit on a couch near the entrance but veered toward the water cooler nearby. She took a paper cone of water then went to her initial destination. As she sat down, clasping her white cane between her knees, a woman in a yellow parka came down a set of stairs and got herself a cone of water as well.

She smiled at Evergreen and sat beside her on the couch.

"Good day, sister," the woman greeted Evergreen.

"Good morning," Evergreen said politely.

"Your expression says you've seen better days," the woman said.

Evergreen's eyebrows pulled together. She'd never been good at schooling her expressions, but she wasn't used to getting called out for it either. On the other hand, she was quite used to people approaching her and telling her their life stories. She steeled herself for the tale she knew was coming.

"You know what always makes me feel better when I'm feeling out of sorts?" the woman asked.

"What?" Evergreen knew she didn't really have to ask, but she didn't want to be rude.

"The Word. Have you heard the Word, sister?"

Here we go, Evergreen thought, internalizing her sigh. "Yes," she told the woman. "I've heard the word."

The woman smiled openly, and Evergreen found it hard to be irritated in the face of such friendliness. "Then you *know*. I'm sorry you're having a rough time right now. Would you like to pray for strength with me?"

"No, thank you. No offense, but I'm not Christian."

The woman tilted her head at her, her brow crinkled. "But you said you knew the Word…"

Evergreen had met with this sort of confusion before, someone who thought that if you understood what Jesus was saying, you surely would follow him. If you didn't follow him, then you must not understand. "You asked if I'd heard the word. Yes, I have heard the word, and I understand it. But that doesn't mean I agree with it. That doesn't mean it speaks to me."

Her confusion still palpable, the woman offered herself an explanation. "Perhaps, it just hasn't been expressed to you properly."

Evergreen shook her head gently. "Let me put it to you this way: you know that feeling you get when you go to church or read the bible? That feeling of belonging, of light, of hope, of peace?"

She nodded.

"I get that feeling, too. But I don't get it from going to church or reading the bible. I get it from walking in the woods, from beating a drum. The old gods give me that feeling. I don't even know you, but as one human being to another, I know how special that feeling is. I would never try to take that feeling away from you. And as a woman who clearly cares for others, I would expect you to have enough empathy to not try to take that feeling away from me."

The woman's face was serious as she carefully considered Evergreen's words. "I understand," she said finally. "I'm glad you have found that sort of light in your life. So many are lost and looking for hope. May you have peace whatever path you walk on, sister."

Evergreen sighed in relief, glad she had reached someone, glad she had met an open heart who understood. "Thank you. I'm glad you have something to get you through as well."

Just as Evergreen and the woman shared a warm smile, the others returned. Evergreen stood from the couch and nodded at the woman.

"Happy holidays," the woman said.

"Happy holidays," Evergreen responded.

CHAPTER 42

Sawyer went back out to Wes's car to get the last of the groceries. Just as he slipped his hands into the handles of the cloth bags, he heard footsteps behind him, crunching the snow as they approached.

"I've got the rest," Sawyer said. "But if you could shut the trunk, that would be…"

His words trailed off as he turned around and saw Eeva standing before him.

"Sawyer…" she started, her voice soft but clear.

He flinched at the sound he'd begged for only days prior.

"I need to—"

"I have to get these things inside," Sawyer cut her off mid-sentence.

"It's not as if anything will melt," she argued. "Don't you have a second?"

Sawyer shook his head. *I can't do this,* he thought, his chest squeezing his lungs so tight it was hard to breathe. "Whatever it is, I'm sure someone else can help you with it."

As he walked past her, his mind shouted that he wanted to know what was so important that she would approach him. *What could possibly make her ask me for something? Is it the same thing she wanted last night?* His mind wanted to know, but his heart didn't. His heart couldn't handle her saying his name, couldn't handle her voice in his ears, couldn't handle her eyes on him. It was good, old fashioned, self-preservation that made him leave her outside without looking back.

Sawyer didn't know what he'd been expecting when he'd brushed Eeva off. If he'd thought she would give up and leave him alone, he had been sorely mistaken.

For the rest of the day, she watched him, looking for any chance to get him alone. But he was not the same old Sawyer who would just give in. He couldn't be. And though he wanted nothing more than to take a long walk alone in the woods to ground his emotions, he didn't dare. He couldn't afford the possibility that she would follow him. He could barely handle being in the same room with her with the rest of the coven there. He knew if he heard her call to him again, he'd be even more pathetic than he was now.

As it was, he knew he was hardly holding it together. He knew he would be a wreck once he got home. But at least he could be a wreck all by himself. *I don't want to ruin anyone else's Yule by being all depressed and miserable,* he thought as he narrowly missed being alone with her in the kitchen. *Can't she see that?*

As Sawyer lay on the couch again that night, he counted

how many hours he would have to get through before he could leave. A shuffling from the hallway made Sawyer close his eyes.

"Sawyer?" Eeva murmured.

He didn't open them, gritting his teeth against the wave of despair that her whisper brought.

The shuffling grew louder. "Are you asleep?" she asked.

He could feel the weight of her presence hanging over him as she got close enough to see whether his eyes were closed. He kept still.

She sighed and shuffled back from whence she'd come.

So what if I'm a coward for not wanting to face her, he thought. *She ripped my heart out and lit it on fire. She doesn't even seem to notice how all this is affecting me. So yeah, I pretended to be asleep to get out of talking to her. What is there left to say anyway? She regrets the best thing that has ever happened to me. The thing I longed for the better part of a decade. It's going to take me more than a few days to get over it.*

Sawyer's phone dinged with another message from the group chat. His coworkers were still sharing their holiday fun. He sighed and put his phone on silent.

The following day was set to be a long one. Wes would begin the bulk of his Yule cooking. Everyone would make their Yule charms. And, that evening, they would stay up through the longest night of the year until dawn, as was tradition.

A hum of excitement hung over the group, though they would all probably take a nap sometime in the afternoon so they could stay up all night.

Eeva was still trying to get Sawyer's attention, and Sawyer was still ignoring her, though it got more and more difficult as time went on. After lunch, Dorian brought out the stuff for everyone to make their Yule charms.

"Everyone have their green cloth and red string?" he asked.

They nodded, and Wes placed a big mortar and pestle on the dining room table in front of him.

"All right. This charm is for us to attune to the sun energy that is on the rise. We have bay, cinnamon, and nutmeg." He dropped equal parts of the herbs and spices into the mortar and began crushing them with the pestle. "Now, when we light our candles during the Yule ritual tomorrow, we're going to make wishes. But feel free to put some energy into this if there is something you want to manifest."

After Dorian had pulverized the ingredients to his satisfaction, he reached into the mortar and took some of the mixture. Then, he placed it at the center of his green cloth and tied it into a sachet with the red string. He passed the mortar to his left so everyone could take some.

When it reached Sawyer, he took some of the powder and sprinkled it on his cloth. He thought of all the energies associated with the sun. *The fiery energy of the sun offers guidance and enlightenment on matters of the heart,* he thought. *This is what I ask for.*

He tied the green cloth with the red string and put the sachet in his pocket.

CHAPTER 43

After they had made the Yule charms, they split off into smaller groups. Wes had asked Devan and Cory if they wouldn't mind going into the garage to drill the candle holes into the Yule log. The Yule log would act as a centerpiece during the celebration the following day until the candles burned down to their nubs. Then they would burn the log in the fireplace, saving only a small piece to light next year's Yule fire. Sawyer got up without a word to join them.

"Sawyer," Evergreen called out to him. Her time was running out, and she had less and less luxury to try to speak to him alone.

Tara, Cassandra, and Hazel, who were sitting on the couch, looked over at him. Evergreen kept her smile internal when he turned back to her, the peacemaker inside him unable to snub her with an audience.

"I'm still not comfortable with the holly king and oak king

dance, and it's tomorrow. Do you mind going over it with me one more time?"

Evergreen couldn't see his face, but she could feel his frustration at having been cornered.

"You were fine the other day," he hedged.

"Well, we never finished the other day, and I want to make sure I get the last part down."

He sighed. "Yeah, all right."

"The meditation room is free, and it's pretty cold outside. Let's go in there," Evergreen suggested.

She led the way, and he pushed their sleeping bags to the side to make room before he faced her.

"Where are the staves?" he asked, looking around when she wasn't holding them.

Evergreen paused for a moment. "I lied about the dance," she murmured. "I just wanted to talk to you, and I didn't know another way of getting you alone."

Sawyer turned on his heel to leave without a word.

Panic lurched in Evergreen's stomach and climbed up her throat. "It wasn't a mistake," she said in a rush to get it out before he could leave.

Sawyer froze but didn't turn back to face her.

She tried to get out as much as she could while she still had time. "I accidentally saw a text on your phone and thought it was from your girlfriend. I don't regret what happened between us. The truth…the truth is I've been wanting it to happen for a long time, practically as long as I've known you."

There was a heavy silence, and Evergreen continued, her voice softer but still audible. "I love you, Sawyer." She laughed bitterly at herself. "I've always loved you. I'm so—"

Her apology was cut off as Sawyer spun around and crushed his mouth to hers. A relieved ache welled up in her chest, and tears rolled down her cheeks as she pulled him closer. A half sigh, half sob escaped her lips, and Sawyer broke their kiss, resting his forehead against hers.

"Don't cry, Eeva," he murmured, wiping her tears away. "I love you, too. I've loved you since I was a stupid teenage boy too shy to tell you how I felt."

Evergreen inhaled a shaky breath, his words making her tears flow harder. "Is that true?" she asked, her voice thick and nasally as her nose stuffed.

"It is," he assured, his amber eyes serious and true as he stared into hers.

She smiled through her tears. "I thought I'd fucked it all up," she told him. "I thought you'd never talk to me again."

He hushed her soothingly, stroking her hair.

Her breathing gradually evened out, and her eyes dried. "Will you kiss me again?" she murmured.

His smile warmed her chest.

"As many times as you want."

Sawyer kissed her sweetly, kissed her gently. And he continued to kiss her until her heated blood wanted more.

"Lock the door," she urged as she gasped for air.

He was gone but a moment, and then he was back with his arms around her as he trailed his lips down her neck.

He lifted her off her feet, and she wrapped her legs around him. His hot body pressed her against the cold glass of the meditation room wall as he drowned her in kisses.

"Do you have a condom?" he asked against her neck, his

breath fogging up the window as he ground his ready cock against her equally ready core.

"Do you think we're the kind of Pagans who don't have contraceptives in the altar room?" she countered with a smirk.

"Where?" His voice was deep and husky, urgent.

The sound raised the hairs on her neck and arms, making her shiver. "In the cabinet," she breathed.

He didn't leave her but carried her over to the altar and laid her down before it, twisting at the torso to reach into the altar cabinet without having to untangle himself from her legs.

But as Sawyer fumbled with the wrapper, Evergreen released his torso and removed her pants and underwear. Before she'd even fully let go of the fabric, Sawyer slid deep inside her.

She gasped, and he smothered her moan with his mouth. Her mind went fuzzy as he settled atop her, his weight solid and real on her chest. Once he was inside her, he slowed to a steady rock, his face hovering over hers so she could see every smile, every bite of the lip, every loving glance from his amber eyes.

Evergreen had a hard time keeping quiet as Sawyer led her to her peak. But once they were finished, she was too satiated to care if anyone had heard her as Sawyer fluttered kisses on her face and neck.

"I have so much to tell you," she murmured, as she lay in his arms atop one of the sleeping bags.

"We have more than enough time," he assured. "Even when we leave, we can see each other after work and on the weekends. You don't have to rush to say everything at once."

Evergreen pulled back, frowning. "But how are we going to see each other that often? You live so far away."

"No, I don't," he informed. "I live in Marshton same as you."

Evergreen sat up and looked down at him. "What? When? How?" she demanded.

"I moved there last year when I got the job at the rehabilitation center."

Evergreen's eyes still held many questions.

Sawyer chuckled, pulling her down to him and kissing her on the mouth. "We have time," he repeated.

CHAPTER 44

"We should probably head out there. Don't you think?" Eeva said, not making a move to back up her statement. "It's already dark out. Even if they took naps to be able to stay up all night, they would be awake by now."

Sawyer tightening his arms around her. "We don't have to," he said with a tone of finality.

Eeva giggled, the sound making his heart feel light. "We're supposed to be spending Yule together with everybody."

"Yule is tomorrow. We can spend it with everyone tomorrow. Nope. I've shared you with them too long already."

Eeva smiled, snuggling in closer to him. "As long as you don't think anyone will come knocking."

"Your mom is the one who told us to lock the door," he said.

"That's true." She laughed.

They were both quiet for a moment before Eeva said, "It's a little early, but can I give you your Yule present now?"

Sawyer pulled away, glancing down at her. "Did you get me a gift?"

She smiled and nodded. Then she wiggled out of his arms and went to her suitcase. He sat up as she dug through. She returned shortly after with a paper shopping bag from Toil and Trouble.

"Open it," she urged, holding it out to him.

He felt himself grin as his heart squeezed in anticipation. He pulled out the tissue paper and reached into the bag. His fingers closed around a cool metal object. He took it out.

A shiny copper pentacle hung on a smooth black cord.

"It's to replace the one you gave to Sol. I think this one suits you better, too. The copper will go so nice with your hair color."

He clasped the necklace around his neck. "Thank you, Eeva," he said earnestly. "I love it."

Her answering smile was an even better gift. "I know I was being kind of a brat before we all went shopping. So don't worry about getting me anything."

Sawyer tilted his head. "What makes you think I don't already have something for you?" he asked. He went over to his bag and got Eeva's gifts before returning and setting them out before her.

She raised her eyebrows. "What? So many? You didn't have to."

"Oh, these aren't all from this year. I got you a gift every year…" he trailed off, suddenly embarrassed.

Her smile widened. "You did?"

He nodded, trying to ignore the slight heat he felt in his cheeks.

"Which was the one from the first year?" she asked.

He stared down at the packages and pointed at the small packet wrapped in what was once a brown paper bag.

She unwrapped it, and pulled out the quartz pendulum he'd gotten her his first Yule away.

"It has stones for each of the chakras," he told her. "And it has a clasp at the end, so you can wear it as a bracelet, too."

"It's adorable," she complimented.

"This one is next," he said before she was even done admiring her first gift. He offered her the one that was most square.

She unwrapped it, revealing a coffee cup that read, "Hex the Patriarchy." Her lips mouthed the words, and she burst out laughing.

His chest warmed at the sound. "I knew you'd like that," he said. "Now this one." He handed her the squishiest one.

She put the mug down beside her and unwrapped the red drawstring bag. "What's in here?" she asked, opening the bag. "Oh!" she gasped. "Did you make these?"

He nodded as she shook some of the wooden runes into her palm.

"They're beautiful!" she exclaimed. "My very own runes. You're going to have to help me practice."

"I will," he promised.

"Is this one next?" she pointed at the rectangle one beside the Toil and Trouble bag.

"Yes."

She gasped when she unwrapped the hand-carved tarot box he'd made. "Sawyer, how long did this take you? It's gorgeous."

Sawyer shrugged, embarrassed but pleased at her reaction. "Last one," he urged, pushing the bag toward her.

"I feel spoiled already," she said with a smile, reaching her hand into the bag and pulling out the mistletoe hairpin.

"Clover said it was real mistletoe," he explained as she smiled and stroked the smooth resin.

"Is it?" she asked, dangling the hairpin over her head and raising her eyebrows at him expectantly.

He leaned over and kissed her once, twice, five times, one for every Yule since he'd last seen her.

Eeva snuggled up beside him, resting her head on his shoulder. They sat like that for a while, quiet and comfortable in each other's company. Then, she slipped her hand under his shirt. He shivered as she stroked his stomach slow and deliberate.

"You know," she murmured. "I'm not very good at staying up all night. I think you're going to have to keep me occupied so I don't fall asleep."

Sawyer's manhood stiffened. "How many hours until dawn?" he asked.

"Hmm, longest night of the year? Give or take fourteen hours."

"I'm going to be honest with you. I might have to take some breaks, but I'm willing to try my very best."

"I believe in you," she murmured right before she pressed a hungry kiss to his lips.

By the time the eastern horizon started to lighten on December the twenty-first, Sawyer felt confident he'd made up for not being honest with Eeva for all those years.

They pulled on their rumpled clothes and shuffled to the

living room like two creatures emerging from a winter's long hibernation.

"Where is everyone?" Eeva asked, blinking at the empty room.

Sawyer poked his head into the kitchen. And though he was greeted with the mouthwatering scent of glazed ham and spiced, he didn't see anyone.

"Sawyer?" Eeva called him from the front hall.

He met her there where he found a cowbell and a tambourine beside the door.

"They must already be outside," she said.

"It's almost time," he agreed.

They pulled on their coats, hats, and boots then grabbed the instruments before heading out the front door.

Eeva slipped her arm into Sawyer's, using him as a guide in the still-dark morning.

"Watch the steps," he told her as he led her off the porch and around to the side of the house.

They found the coven huddled in their coats and hoods, their eyes trained on the eastern horizon.

Just as Sawyer and Eeva settled in behind them, the sun shone its first light.

"There it is!" Sol shouted, pointing at the first rays of dawn.

Everyone responded in a burst of noise. They hollered and whooped. They banged their drums and shook their bells. They greeted the sun, the newly reborn god, with cries of welcome.

And as he shook his cowbell and Eeva jingled her tambourine, he smiled over at her. Her face was open and bright in the morning sunshine. He couldn't help but lean down and press a kiss to her smiling lips.

The cheers of the coven turned to whistles and laughs.

"I have a feeling we will be meeting sooner rather than later," Devan said, chuckling.

"I see a handfasting in our future," Piper added.

"Finally!" Cassandra shouted.

"I know," Tara agreed. "It's about damn time."

Eeva broke their kiss, burying her face in his chest.

"Don't say finally," Sawyer argued with a grin. "Finally makes it sound like the end. It's a new day, a new season. We're only just beginning."

If you enjoyed *A Very Witchy Yuletide*, please leave a review to help other readers decide on this book!

If you'd like to be notified when D. Lieber releases new books, sign up for the newsletter at www.dlieber.com

ALSO BY D. LIEBER

Conjuring Zephyr

The Exiled Otherkin

Intended Bondmates

In Search of a Witch's Soul, Council of Covens Noir, #1

Dancing with Shades, Council of Covens Noir, #0

Once in a Black Moon

The Fanciful Travels of D. Lieber

ABOUT THE AUTHOR

D. Lieber is an urban fantasy author with a wanderlust that would make a butterfly envious. When she isn't planning her next physical adventure, she's recklessly jumping from one fictional world to another. Her love of reading led her to earn a Bachelor's in English from Wright State University.

Beyond her skeptic and slightly pessimistic mind, Lieber wants to believe. She has been many places—from Canada to England, France to Italy, Germany to Russia—believing that a better world comes from putting a face on "other." She is a romantic idealist at heart, always fighting to keep her feet on the ground and her head in the clouds.

Lieber lives in Wisconsin with her husband (John) and cats (Yin and Nox).

Links
  Website: www.dlieber.com
  Twitter: www.twitter.com/AuthorDLieber
  Goodreads: www.goodreads.com/dlieberwriting
  Bookbub: www.bookbub.com/profile/d-lieber

Lightning Source UK Ltd.
Milton Keynes UK
UKHW012010281020
372399UK00003B/7/J